"A disturbing story with echoes of past conflicts. Few of us want to remember the fall of Saigon; none of us wants to encounter the countess again."

- Andrew Trumbull

"The convoluted morality of this story disturbed me enough to send me back to Milton. (Massachusetts, not John; I needed to go home, and feel safe again.)

- Morris Quint

"I'd rather have lunch with Lucrezia Borgia."

- The author's mother

ISBN-13: 978-1978252271

ISBN-10: 1978252277

ii

The Countess Comes Home

a novel

by

Michael Reidy

Lattimer & Co.

PHILADELPHIA · LONDON · PARIS

2019

For Rachel
who doesn't do lunch

Author's note

There are many tales of bravery, dedication, heroism, and sacrifice from the War in Vietnam.

This is not one of them.

There is little action in this story, apart from some clandestine operations and moral acrobatics. The drama, such as it is, falls into that grey area where the operational, political, and diplomatic blur: in short, the sort of work that ordinary servicemen were asked to undertake on a regular basis.

Bill Bradley, the hero of this story, is not to be compared to the tens of thousands who unwillingly served in dangerous combat roles. He, himself, would admit that his greatest fear while on Yankee Station and in Saigon, from October 1972 until April 1973 was being discovered for the incompetent he was.

For Bill Bradley, it was the countess who dominated; who pulled the strings, and made his life interesting for a few months.

Nonetheless, Bill Bradley's war was as real to him as other soldiers' wars were to them. Fear was omnipresent, and Death was near. His war just seemed to be taking place in a parallel universe.

Belladonna, n.: In Italian, a beautiful lady; in English, a deadly poison. A striking example of the essential identity of the two tongues.

- Ambrose Bierce

The Countess Comes Home

Chapter I

It had been more than a decade since I'd heard from Osgood. I thought he might be dead; he was certainly retired, but then, the familiar, small, white envelope arrived with the government frank printed on it. Otherwise, there was nothing on the envelope except my name and address, written with a fountain pen. It was the same way his predecessor communicated with me.

Slitting it open, I found the familiar Ministry of Defence insignia, and a short, handwritten note that had a date, a time and place above the signature, "Osgood."

So, Osgood was still alive, and able to get around. It didn't matter whether I was busy on the day he proposed; I simply had to be there.

A long time had passed since I received such orders. Osgood's name was one of the only ones that could still make me jump. I didn't resent it because it had always been part of the job. Unconventional, to be sure, but, as they say, it had its moments.

Osgood proposed 11.00 a.m., the following Tuesday at his club in Pall Mall. I'd been there before, many times, going back as many years; it is where we had our briefing and debriefing sessions. I knew Osgood to be older than I, and I had been retired for several years. The business we had together reached back far farther than my acquaintance with Osgood. I didn't meet him for more than a decade after the events that would be the focus of our discussion. We had done many projects since, but "*L'affaire de la Comtesse,*" as he always referred to it, was the only one that anyone *ever* wanted to talk about.

Osgood had replaced Hawthorne. While I considered Osgood to be "old school," Hawthorne was even older school. His self-parodying and dapper, if anachronistic, style, belied a mind that was as organised as the Bodleian Library, and as comprehensive. He was masterful at getting information while revealing nothing.

By the time Osgood took over, I was more experienced in dealing with such people, but by then, no one really cared about those earlier days. As a result, Osgood revealed a good deal more, though still not enough for a full picture.

I'd always have questions. Why I had been chosen? What was in the envelopes I delivered? Was any of it worth the trouble and subterfuge? And, I had lots of questions of my own about the countess.

Though Osgood and I would talk for hours, I'd probably leave feeling I knew little more than when I arrived.

The Countess Comes Home

so

On the appointed day, I travelled up from deepest Sussex and walked to Pall Mall, making a stop at my bank in Trafalgar Square. Although I hadn't been there in over a year, I was greeted by name, and cashed a small cheque. I wouldn't need much, because the club will bill Osgood, and he will pass it to the ministry.

The club, which I had originally thought imposing, was now looking tired and worn. Its visible members were yesterday's men, not today's, nor tomorrow's. If the stories were true, "yesterday" had been an interesting time for the club. There were rumours of war-time interrogations in the basement, and even the odd execution. However, the food was still good, so it remained a pleasant enough place to visit, at someone else's expense, as long as one was certain of being able to walk out the door unassisted.

Osgood, himself, showed fewer signs of decay. Greyer; less hair, and more weight, but otherwise upright, animated, and still slightly sinister.

After greeting each other, he proposed that we go directly to lunch, over which we discussed our health; our families; where we'd travelled recently; what we'd seen and read; the state of the world, and British politics.

Like most things we do, this follows ministry protocol. It was designed to appear neutral, but was formulated so

3

long ago that it now has the opposite effect. It is a ritual designed to keep encounters between operatives as impersonal as possible, to make ordering someone on a certain-death mission (or, just pulling the trigger yourself) easier. Throw in the odd "old boy," and all would run smoothly.

What made it trickier for Osgood was that I'm an American, and have a higher sense of self-worth than British operatives do. I think it's because, as citizens, not subjects, we are less apt to do as we're told, unquestioningly.

The British have called themselves "citizens" since the John Major days, but it hasn't changed how they act, or, for that matter, what they are.

Osgood and I had a gin and tonic before our meal, which ran to three courses, and a bottle of claret, before we started on the coffee and brandy. Some government agencies still do things properly. The main reason this one does is because most people believe it was disbanded in 1940.

Not until we were on the second pot of coffee, and were left with the brandy bottle, did Osgood raise the matter of the countess.

"There's the odd chance of an old ghost and a few skeletons coming out of the cupboard," he began.

"Ones that will bother us?" I asked.

"Very possibly. More to the point, it will bother people for whom being bothered is not good for us," he said. "You know what they say in the Circus: no one is ever truly dead."

"But you weren't in the Circus, and I was never with the Company," I said.

Osgood's face tensed and he sucked air through his teeth the way tradesmen do before they tell you that something's going to cost an extra five hundred pounds.

"Not *technically*," he said. "It would be hard to *prove* where the money came from that paid for your little operation, but it does have the whiff of greasepaint and sawdust about it."

I laughed, too loudly for the surroundings, but the great room was empty, even of staff, so there was only Osgood to upset, and he didn't seem bothered.

"*My* operation?" I exclaimed. "I was a mere functionary."

"'Just following orders,'" he said. "That didn't work then, and it won't work now."

"Just to be clear, we *are* talking about the countess, aren't we?" I asked. "I mean, just in case some other superficially innocent activity I participated in decades ago was another pear-shaped MI7 project."

"You know that agency no longer exists," he said gently, but firmly.

"How old are you, Osgood? Seventy-two? Seventy-four? I'm sixty-seven," I protested. "No one's going to come after us."

"Tell that to John Damjanjuk."

I threw my napkin on the table, and sat back in my chair about to stand up.

"I delivered what I was told were radio scripts – probably propaganda – from MI7 to the American radio station via the countess where the British weren't supposed to be operating. That's it," I said. "I don't know what else your crowd got up to, but you're not getting me involved again!"

I stood up.

Osgood did nothing for a moment, and continued to stare at the table cloth.

"You haven't finished your brandy," he said calmly. "It really is worth finishing."

I sat down again. Having never been more than a junior officer, I was still susceptible to doing what I was told.

Osgood's manner didn't change, but his voice went very quiet.

"Messages have been received that the countess wants to come home," he said.

I stared at him. No doubt, I looked a fool, with wide eyes, and possibly open mouth.

"Has someone heard from her?" I was eventually able to ask.

"I don't know."

Which meant, I'm not going to tell you.

He read my thoughts and chuckled.

"I really don't know," he said with a smile. "I'm as far out of things as you are. All I know is that I was told that a message came through our embassy in Paris requesting permission to return to the UK."

This didn't ring true on several counts. I suspected that Osgood wanted me to question this as methodically, and pedantically as I would have done were I being paid.

"'A message came through,'" I began. "That implies that it didn't come from the countess. So, who did it come from?"

Osgood gave the hint of a smile.

"Good," he said. "Someone acting on her behalf."

"Obviously," I said.

"Anything else?" he prompted.

"'Return to the UK,'" I replied. "The countess had French and South Vietnamese citizenship. Then, the ministry gave her an Italian passport – but in another name."

Osgood sipped his brandy, and nodded.

"Presumably, both the French and Italian passports were converted to EU passports in the 1990s," I reasoned on the fly. "That would give her the right to enter the UK, but it doesn't explain the notion of 'returning.'"

"Not bad, Bradley," Osgood said. "Anything more?"

"This puzzled me at the time," I said. "The countess' father was British. That could make her eligible for British citizenship. She may have been registered at birth. However, as I remember, he never lived in the United Kingdom. He may never have visited here. He was born in Hong Kong, India, or some British-Asian territory, and as a result of his, shall we say, *unusual*, activities, may have even lost his passport; but was the countess ever considered British?"

Osgood nodded again, and waited for me to puzzle out the next stage.

My brain was working on the question, while at the same time telling me to stop playing silly games; thank Osgood for lunch, and head back to Charing Cross.

"Ah!" I said, after a few minutes. "I do see one possibility, possibly two.

"First, someone in MI7 must have known she was British, too, and that's why they engaged her. She wasn't an embassy secretary asked to do some extra work; she was deliberately recruited. I don't think she was doing much of anything then, apart from shopping with friends – not that I ever met any of them.

"The second possibility is that she was an unwilling pawn, used to pay back the British, or redeem her father," I said. "He got himself into some scrape, and either needed rescuing, or some *quid pro quo* to get him off the hook; or, he was negotiating for her safety when the balloon went up."

I paused to think some more.

"So, why did she not come back to Britain then? Why be placed under a loose house arrest in a God-forsaken town in Italy? – unless, what she had done in Vietnam was something they didn't want to come out."

"Bravo!" Osgood said. "We are beginning at the same point."

The countess had been gone for a long time; to want to come back now would be a big change. What I did know is that MI-whatever would not want awkward questions raised. Statutes of limitations would have lapsed, and freedom of information legislation would make it relatively easy to have any documents released.

Osgood must know a lot more than I. I thought the countess was safe, settled and forgotten. Apparently not.

"I've re-read the file, not that there is much," he said. "Now I want to hear all that you know."

"More like all I remember," I said. "I haven't thought much about it for a long time, and what does it matter what I remember?"

"You remember where she was, don't you?" he asked.

"Up to a point. I took her to Italy," I said. "Did some other operative or agency move her?"

"We think she is not there anymore," Osgood said.

I sat up and became more alert.

"That was the deal; that she remain in Italy," I said.

"Yes," Osgood agreed. "Apparently, she hasn't been in Italy for years."

"But you don't know," I tested.

"No."

"And the money – "

"The money goes into a London bank. It always has; just like yours," he said.

"Mine stopped in 1985."

He ignored this pointed reminder.

"The money was then automatically transferred to a bank in Stigliano, where it was almost immediately withdrawn," he said.

"She needed to live."

He didn't reply.

"So, she is still being paid?" I asked.

Osgood made a gesture to suggest he didn't know.

"Banco Puttanesca, or whatever it was, was taken over in 2009, and the new bank won't tell us," he said. "It's run by a very left-wing group that doesn't want to cooperate with foreign capitalists."

"What you're saying is that you've lost the countess?"

"I prefer to say the countess has become lost," Osgood grudgingly admitted. "Worse, most of the paperwork can't be found, either."

"In the best MI7 tradition." I said, barely able to keep from laughing.

"Can we try to keep this civil," Osgood said, more hurt than annoyed.

"Can one slander a department that doesn't exist?" I asked. "Oh, Osgood, why does anyone *care*? Why shouldn't she come to the UK and finish her life? She may have been

11

British after all, wasn't she? Are we suddenly getting fussy?"

"Some think there are very good reasons why she shouldn't come back. Some could be very embarrassed – and, no, I don't know who. You and I need to work out why, and who might be – *inconvenienced* – by her return," he said. "Tell me your story again, then we will see if we can lay this to rest."

"Have you been brought back on active duty for this?" I asked.

"Someone obviously thinks it's worth another look," he said.

"And me? Am I on temporary active duty, too?" I asked.

"No."

"So, you get paid, and I don't."

Osgood looked at me, but said nothing.

I helped myself to another brandy.

"Where do you want me to start?"

"At the beginning."

Chapter II

The events leading up to the fall of Saigon were more than forty years ago. Memories of that bitter time are fading, and four decades of conflicts and crises have erased it from the public consciousness. Yet, for those of us who spent any time there, it's a memory that is never far away. To those who lost family, close friends, or were wounded, the pain is constant. For others, like me, the experience, which stood like a hurdle in our early lives, continues to haunt, and anger as the ignorance and insensitivity of the present fails to recognise the significance of that war to a generation.

All right. No more of this pseudo-psycho-historio analysis; it's all been said, and better. My little tale isn't one of the *angst* of the rights and wrongs, but one of how, even in the midst of the confusion of war, there were a few islands of quiet madness.

଼

I've never been anyone remarkable. Not at school; not in college; not in the military, and certainly not in my subsequent career.

If there is any advantage in being one who habitually keeps his head down, it is that one is never suspected of doing anything out of line.

I'm Bill. Bill Bradley. William Francis Bradley. Only son of equally imaginatively named parents, John James Bradley, and Frances Mary Kane. Solid Midwesterners, all of us.

A bit of noticeable achievement in high school and college, but not too much. Tennis. Archery. Not too brainy, but sound, if a little dull. Military, not by choice. Undistinguished, until singled out, randomly; then the pattern broke.

For a few months in Vietnam, I was – apparently – doing something remarkable. Looking back, I can see that it was one of the times I may have got out of line. All right. I *did* get out of line, and with life-long consequences.

The other consequence of looking back, critically, was to see how naïve I was; how little I knew of what was going on around me. I was a part of the war machine; one that wasn't making any real difference; not one who took any risks, but one who got on with his bureaucratic job, and was as culpable as those dropping the bombs.

⚃

I was in my university's last ROTC company before it was banished from the campus, along with the money that enabled people like me to go to college. I took my commission in the Navy, which was more tolerant of degrees in history than the Air Force, or Army.

My studies and naval training would be of little interest to the reader. That's not to say it didn't matter how much I loved history, or how good my essays were: I still ended up on the *USS Harrisburg* in the South China Sea.

The *Harrisburg* was ordered before the end of World War II, and was the only Capital Class (a prototype for the Des Moines class) heavy cruiser to be built. Political arguments about budgets held up construction, but in the end, rather than scrap the two-thirds-finished ship, it was eventually commissioned in 1948. At 20,000 tons (standard), and 725 feet (after conversion), CA-160 was the heaviest cruiser ever built. It justified its existence in Korea, and now, as CG-160, was pulling her weight on Yankee Station in its third WesPac deployment.

In addition to hurling some shells a dozen or so miles, we could launch some rockets as well. For whatever reason, whenever I watched, the missiles would do some interesting corkscrew aerobatics, and then slam into the ocean a few hundred yards from the ship. Perhaps they had some secret anti-submarine capabilities I hadn't been told about.

I was the public affairs officer; just another green (often

literally) ensign among 1,142 officers and men. The public affairs office (PAO) in peace time had a compartment of its own, an officer and two yeomen. Occasionally, there had been a Navy-trained journalist. Since the conversion to a guided missile cruiser, which destroyed a number of office and berthing spaces, PAO and Admin had to share a compartment. To add to the inconvenience, my one man, a sailor training to be a yeoman, broke his leg and was evacuated to Subic Bay. In typical military fashion, he remained "attached to the ship," so, technically, there was no vacancy in the office, and I had to make do without him.

I was grudgingly given part-time use of a reasonably competent yeoman from Admin, but all he had time for was typing clean copies of press releases and reports. I was doing all the writing, and sending out press releases and a few features. I was also standing watches along with every other junior officer aboard, but was never entrusted with anything more than keeping the ship going straight.

That sounds standard fare, but the reality in the military is never as simple. Admin, PAO and the Flag Office (we occasionally had an admiral embarked) had been given new IBM Selectric ("golf ball") typewriters during our last trip stateside. There is no doubt that they were wonderful workhorse machines, producing sharp type and able to be used for producing layouts for printing. The downside was that to do this, they used carbon ribbons that after one use were consigned to the trash. While there had been a generous budget for the few dozen new machines, there was almost nothing allocated for ribbons, with the consequence that by the time we reached Yankee Station, they had all been used.

Supply told me that they had crates of cloth ribbons for manual typewriters, but while this sounded promising, it transpired that the forty-five old typewriters had been dropped over the side. By 1972, air freighting carbon typewriter ribbons to Southeast Asia wasn't high on the Pentagon's list of priorities.

In the great scheme of things, PAO's work would be missed less than Admin's, so my "normal" work ceased, and I began The Great Ribbon Search.

My goal was to get aboard a carrier which would have hundreds of similar typewriters, and thousands of ribbons. Our supply officer had knocked up something that looked like a valid requisition form, and I had several versions with me as I was heloed from one ship to another in the hope of ending up on a carrier.

In fact, it wasn't until the *Harrisburg* was enjoying a respite from the war at Pearl Harbor that ribbons were eventually sourced. In the meantime, someone heard rumours about some typewriters, and a separate investigation was launched.

Two sailors who had been charged with disposing of the manual machines had kept half a dozen hidden in various spare parts lockers with the hopes of selling them when they went on leave. In the best tradition of ordinary sailors, they negotiated a hundred dollars for each machine and freedom from any disciplinary action. The whole transaction came close to falling apart when it was discovered that the supply officer, on hearing that his crates of cloth ribbons were now redundant, had arranged his own back-office sale, and the ribbons were about to be sent to Saigon where the Air Force had its own ribbon crisis. Fortunately, this was discovered before the completion of the deal. (Rumour had it that the supply officer lost out on a new set of golf clubs.)

I, or at least my would-be yeoman, was allowed use of one of the machines, so PAO was back in business.

During my ten days of unsuccessful ship-hopping in mid-September, I had ended up in Sydney, and spent a night aboard a British destroyer, *HMS Surrey*. Most of the junior officers were ashore, so I dined with the captain and a few commanders as well as a gentleman named Hawthorne who had come from London on undisclosed business.

Over a number of drinks, Hawthorne and I discussed various aspects of British history, focusing mostly on the treachery of Walsingham, and the French and British use of spies during the Napoleonic wars. As the officers' knowledge of the latter stretched no further than the Scarlet Pimpernel, Hawthorne and I were left to get on with our stories, and a bottle of whisky.

As it was the first intellectual conversation I'd had since graduating, I made the most of it.

Somehow, I was able to make my 0700 helo and began the long trip back to the *Harrisburg*. I had had time to visit the IBM dealer in Sydney and pick up as many ribbons as I could carry, so I didn't arrive back empty handed.

These incidents are to illustrate the level of my contribution to the war effort.

∾

About a month later, the captain summoned me to his quarters and gave me a set of orders. Orders for junior officers didn't usually come from the captain, so I was braced for some altercation. While undistinguished, I did not think I'd done anything wrong.

"It appears you're leaving us," he said.

"I'm sorry to hear that, sir," I said.

He looked at me doubtfully.

"You're to report to the *USS Enterprise* for further assignment," he said. "God knows what they've got planned for
you. You haven't pissed anyone off, have you?"

"Only on this ship, sir."

He nodded.

"Well, I hope not too badly. I have been told you will
probably return. Dismissed."

The period between orders is always difficult, especially
if one continues to travel with little idea of the final destination. I was aboard the *Enterprise* for two days, and
then flown off in a decrepit C-1A Trader used for carrier
on-board delivery and personnel transfer. I was headed
to Saigon. After landing at Tan Son Nhut, I was driven to
a BOQ and given a room not much larger than my stateroom on the *Harrisburg*.

There were no messages for me, so I wandered over to the
Personnel Office, eventually found the office that handled the Navy, and asked if they had anything for me.

The personnelman handled a lot of Marine records, but
few for the Navy.

"No, sir. I have nothing," he said. "What were you expecting?"

"Orders."

"I guess all you can do is wait for something to come in."

Apart from the heat, humidity and noise, and the threat of being bombed, the BOQ proved comfortable enough. Better still was the Vietnamese Officers' Club which offered decent food, a swimming pool and an air-conditioned movie theatre. You had to bring your own booze, but the BX was next door, so it provided some exercise, and broke up the day. Inevitably, there were a lot of flyboys, but they had their own club. I found a few other junior officers who did things at my level of importance, and we bowled, swam and drank together.

I spent ten days sitting in the sun, drinking coffee in the morning, beer in the afternoon, and reading endless books and magazines. Each morning and afternoon, I checked in with Personnel, but no orders arrived.

On the eleventh day, the situation changed.

"Looks like you're going back to sea, sir," Grabowsky said. (By then we were on close "Mr Bradley" and "Grabowsky" terms.)

I read the orders. I was to be flown to the *USS America,* and then transferred back to the *USS Harrisburg.* Was this supposed to be R&R? As my flight to the *America* wasn't for three days, I thought I'd abandon my place next to the swimming pool, and venture into the city in the morning.

That evening, while I was having dinner, one of the sergeants, who acted as the receptionist/general factotum for the BOQ, came across to the mess and gave me an envelope.

"Left for you, sir," he said, and departed.

The envelope had my name hand-written on it in green ink, and nothing else.

The note was on a relatively small piece of white paper but had a variant of the royal crest, complete with lion and unicorn. I knew from my historical research that this was from some government department, but I couldn't tell which.

> *Dear Lieutenant Bradley,*
>
> *I enjoyed our conversation aboard* HMS Surrey.
> *Having spoken to various liaison offices from*
> *Hong Kong, you have been attached TAD to our*
> *office to undertake special projects.*
>
> *I look forward to seeing you at the Hoàn-Mỹ (Per-*
> *fection) hotel at 1200 tomorrow. (It says "Majes-*
> *tic" on the top.)*
>
> *Sincerely,*
>
> *Hawthorne*

Well, I assumed it said "Hawthorne," for it was just a scribble following a large "H."

I was too relieved that someone was breaking the boredom to worry too much about what he might want. I spent the rest of the day in or around the swimming pool, listening to the noise of the dozens of planes whose purpose I did not wish to contemplate.

৪৩

In the morning, I hitched a lift into the city with an Army major and a captain who had all the bored weariness of men coming to the end of their time in Vietnam. They were at once laid-back and edgy; nonchalant and alert. They regarded me with distaste as both a rookie and a Navy man, and I found it hard to blame them. I had done nothing for a week except spend my allowance on food and drink, lie in the sun, and make occasional fatuous conversation. I did, however, try to do those things with the demeanour of an officer and a gentleman.

The open Jeep had no suspension, but my companions and the driver expressed no discomfort, rather as a good rider appears to become part of the horse. For half an hour, we rattled over the streets, frequently braking suddenly for pedestrians, bicycles, and mopeds.

There were thousands of people, all apparently with places to go. They looked healthy, well-dressed, and friendly. The bright *áo dài* worn by the women flapped in the breeze making the random movement look choreographed. The colours, after months surrounded by grey, and more recently olive drab and khaki, reminded me that there was more to life than typewriter ribbons, and waiting for orders, even here.

The major did not tell me where they were going, but dropped me by a 1950s-looking shopping centre, quaintly mis-named Eden.

"This is Tu Do," he said, waving his arm up and down the busy street. "The cathedral's that way; the hotel, that way. Enjoy your stay."

I got out, and the Jeep sped off, not giving me the chance to ask how I was to get back.

There was about forty-five minutes before I was scheduled to meet Hawthorne. I had a quick walk through the Eden. It was moderately busy, but the clientele was much different than that I'd seen on the street on the way into the city.

There were westerners; some US military; and smartly-dressed Vietnamese. I could have been in Cleveland. After a quick look around the ground floor, I went back out onto Tu Do and walked up to the cathedral.

Notre Dame Cathedral looked like it had been transplanted from a small French city. Victorian gothic architecture, with round arches and a very high ceiling, gave it

European grandeur, while thousands of memorial and plaques expressing gratitude with Vietnamese inscriptions demonstrated native devotion. It was interesting inasmuch as it demonstrated the conviction of the colonials. The French, in particular, considered their overseas possessions as fully French, not second-class outposts.

A friend had told me that it was not uncommon, on French civil service examinations, to find the question, "France is bordered by all but which of the following countries: Spain, Belgium, the Netherlands, Italy, Brazil?" The odd one out is the Netherlands.

I appreciated the quiet sanctuary of the cathedral, and when I stepped out into the noise, heat and light, I nearly retreated back inside, but it was time to make my way to the Hoàn-Mỹ.

I was surprised to see the river opposite the hotel. In fact, I was surprised to see *any* river, such was my ignorance.

As I entered the hotel – another survivor from an earlier age – I wondered where I should meet Hawthorne. It was a large place with an uneasy blend of the *belle époque*, art deco, and the modern. Plastic or silk flowers had replaced potted palms, and I didn't see a clock that was actually working. Still, the staff made it feel that nothing was amiss; the decay was the illusion and the reality was that all was as it should be.

I decided to go into the bar. It seemed the logical place to look for someone on a hot day. The place was hardly busy. Those people that I saw looked like they had been residents for several decades, and as I surveyed the bar, I would not have been surprised to see Somerset Maugham, Noel Coward, or Joseph Conrad in conversation over cocktails. Indeed, it was just as likely to see Peter Lorre, Humphrey Bogart, or Sydney Greenstreet.

I saw Hawthorne, sitting quietly, impeccably dressed in what I took to be a linen suit, with a panama hat on the seat next to him. He had a copy of the *Times*, and pink gin.

"Good afternoon, Lieutenant," he said, standing to greet me. "I'm glad to see you were able to come."

Hawthorne was very good at pretending that I actually had a choice in what I did.

He gestured to a waiter as he sat down.

"What's your poison?" he asked. "I wouldn't go for the gin and tonic; the gin's fine, but the tonic is unspeakable."

I asked for a beer, hoping it would be cold.

Hawthorne was silent until I was served, and the waiter retreated.

"You probably believe, like most of your countrymen, that we British are uninvolved in the business here," he began. "For the most part, we are; yet, there are things to be done that the Americans can't be seen to be doing. You understand?"

I nodded.

"The awkward thing is, that to be able to do those things, we need to communicate with the Americans, but we can't be seen to be doing that, either," he said with heavy irony. "You see the problem."

Again, I nodded.

"So, what my office needs is the same thing that you Americans need: a go-between."

"And that's going to be me?"

He paused to sip his gin.

"Up to a point, Lord Copper. You will be a part of it."

"A go, or a between?" I asked.

He stared at me, his eyes seldom blinked, but when they did it was as a deliberate act that put one in mind of a tortoise.

"I wouldn't have put it that way, but you've got the idea," he said. "You will be an American go-between for the British, and you will – " he paused to choose the word, "– *liaise* with the British go-between for the Americans."

I said nothing, but tried to work out the logic of it.

"Your note said that I am to work TAD for you, but I received orders back to the ship yesterday," I said.

"Good," he replied. "That's your 'cover', as they say in the films. You will continue doing whatever it is that you do on the *Harrisburg*. From time to time, you will receive instructions to deliver documents to the American go-between, who is British. That's basically it."

"So, I continue to work for the Navy?" I asked.

"That's what it will look like," Hawthorne replied. "When you receive your instructions, they will come like orders, or by comms traffic, your transport will be arranged."

"Transport?"

"You will meet your contact here in Saigon," he said. "Your orders will tell you when and where. Unless your ship is operating within helicopter distance, you will be routed via one of the carriers."

"That can take two days each way," I protested.

"That's all right then," he said easily. "You probably won't have to come more than once a week."

"I won't be able to get my normal work done."

"It's for a good cause," he said.

I hesitated before asking the next question, but Hawthorne appeared to expect it.

"Will I still be paid by the Navy?" I asked.

"Oh, yes," he said. "All that will remain the same: pay; time in rank; pension; insurance; benefits. You will, however, receive an honorarium from Her Majesty's Government. An account will be opened for you at a London bank, and deposits made. Once you are no longer on active duty, you can arrange to transfer the money, or come to the United Kingdom and spend it. What you do about income tax is up to you, but sometimes it's not good to draw attention to yourself."

I thought about this, but Hawthorne pressed on.

"You will be told where to meet your counterpart. Just give her the documents you've been given; do anything else she asks, then make your way back to the ship."

"She?"

"I think you and the countess will get on very well."

After that enigmatic remark, Hawthorne left me. I sat there, alone with my drink in the cavernous bar, wondering what this would mean in practical terms. The waiter came to clear Hawthorne's glass.

"Will you be having lunch, sir?" he asked. "If you follow me, I will take you to a table."

He picked up my glass and took it to a small, round table in what must have once been an elegant dining room. I was able to get a light lunch and some iced tea. My meal was marred only by thoughts about how I was to get back to the air base. Then, I noticed an Air Force colonel at a distant table, also on his own, and conceived a plan.

I waited in the lobby until he came out from the dining room, and turned to him casually.

"Did you enjoy your lunch, sir?"

"Yes, thank you," he said, surprised that I had addressed him.

"Are you headed to the base? Can I get you a car?" I asked.

Now, he was really surprised.

"Are you the hotel liaison?" he asked.

"No, colonel, but I guessed you might be heading to Tan Son Nhut."

"I don't know how you're supposed to get anywhere in this city," he said.

I used the hotel phone to call the motor pool, and requested a car for Colonel Myerson, as his name badge proclaimed him.

"It will be about twenty minutes, Colonel," I told him.

He was sitting at a table near where Hawthorne and I sat.

"Would you like another coffee while you're waiting, sir?"

"What is it that you do, Lieutenant?" he asked.

"Public affairs officer on the *USS Harrisburg*, Colonel."

"You're a bit far from home," he said. "Sit down."

He looked at me.

"I suppose you want to bum a lift with me," he said.

"The motor pool doesn't send cars for JGs."

"There's not much Navy around here," he said.

He went on to say he was forming a unit, and waiting for personnel to arrive. Like me, he had come into the city to see what he could.

I didn't ask him any questions about the new unit, but found he was originally from Colorado, and had been posted all over the US. He hadn't been sent to Vietnam before, and was feeling old to be on his first tour.

After twenty minutes, we went outside to watch for the car, and shortly after, a staff car pulled up. The driver got out and removed the flag from the hood that had two stars on it, and opened the door for the colonel.

The colonel said virtually nothing on the way back to Tan Son Nhut, but he came up to me in the officers' club that evening, and introduced me to two junior officers who looked as green as I was.

One was a captain and the other a first lieutenant. The captain looked dried up already, no doubt from trying to please Colonel Myerson.

We had very little to say to each other, but talked about where we were from; how long we'd been hanging around Tan Son Nhut, and when we expected to get out of Vietnam. By our third beer, we were getting along well, and the colonel left us to it. The others immediately relaxed.

While I was able to talk freely about my work on the *Harrisburg*, I couldn't satisfactorily explain my presence in Saigon, a fact that the captain, in his humourless way, pressed me on.

"Sounds like you're in Naval Intelligence," he said.

"If I told you, you'd have to kill me," I said. "I will have been here two weeks by the time I fly out, and have had one forty-five-minute meeting, the content of which I didn't understand."

The captain nodded.

I looked at the first lieutenant, whose name was Levski.

"I don't have enough rank to be doing anything serious," I said.

"Tell me about it," Levski said. "The trouble is that you have just enough rank to get saddled with any blame."

Chapter III

"Who was Levski?" Osgood asked, picking up on what I thought was the most minor part of my entire narrative.

"When I saw him, I don't think he knew what he was going to be doing," I said. "According to the captain and Lieutenant Levski, they didn't know much about the unit Myerson was setting up, and it's possible neither did he. I gathered from them that the colonel was expecting several more officers, at least two majors, and two or three more captains – some pilots, some not – along with a few dozen men. No one seemed to know where they were."

"What was the captain's name?"

"I'd have to check my journal," I said. "It was a Scandinavian name like Jenson, or Jenssen. His first name was Karl."

Osgood nodded.

"Did it occur to you that they would be doing covert or clandestine work?" he asked.

"No. I thought they were pretty run of the mill guys who

had gone into the Air Force rather than be drafted. Jenssen was keen to fly, but Levski just wanted to go home."

"Family?"

"He was engaged. Betty-Sue," I said, "You couldn't make it up. They were from Ohio, near the Kentucky border. He was another mid-westerner."

Osgood smiled.

"You see what we saved you from."

I gave him a sceptical look.

"Do you think these Air Force boys were relevant in what you did?"

"I didn't then, and, apart from the one subsequent encounter, I don't now," I said. "But, given the convolutions of the work, anything's possible. Butterflies' wings, and all that. Were they important?"

Osgood shifted in his chair.

"Was there anything else of note with your meeting with Hawthorne?" he asked.

"He was minimal in everything he did and said," I said. "There were no superfluous words or actions. It made it difficult to see beyond the obvious."

Osgood thought for a moment, then nodded.

"He had that reputation," he said. "Most people thought he was an accountant. In a way, he was."

We sat in an almost congenial silence for a few minutes. The great dining room remained empty, and I had seen no staff peek in to see if we'd finished.

"Tell me about your first encounter with the countess," Osgood finally said.

௸

The return to the *Harrisburg* took three days. I couldn't get a flight from Saigon to the *Enterprise* until late afternoon, and when we landed, the weather was turning bad. I was put up in one of the carrier's guest suites, which were named after famous hotels. I was in "Enterprise Plaza." I had the suite to myself. It comprised a bedroom with four berths, and a salon with several desks, and a table with chairs for dining, or meetings, and a private head with shower. These suites usually had long-term residents in the form of technical representatives (tech reps) from the aircraft or systems manufacturers.

There was one guest suite on the *Harrisburg* which was periodically occupied by VIPs or DVs (distinguished visitors, not as important as VIPs). As public affairs officer, I had charge of booking them, and ensuring they were ready for instant occupancy. I also had the keys. So far, I had resisted the temptation of using it as a personal office or retreat when the Admin office became too crowded or noisy, but I could see that this new line of work might require some judicious deceit.

The food in the wardroom on the *Enterprise* was very good, but, being a carrier, there was too much brass, and the junior officers vacated as soon as they finished eating, and left the senior officers to their coffee and cigars. So, I found myself back in the suite, alone, by eight o'clock.

I had a number of paperbacks with me, as I knew that whatever this trip brought, it would include a lot of waiting around and time in the air.

I was scheduled to get a helo to the *Harrisburg* around noon the next day, but when I went down for breakfast, a look out the elevator doors on the hangar deck, showed conditions to be rough, with heavy winds and rain. A stop at the Air Transfer Office after breakfast confirmed my fear that there were no non-essential helicopter flights for the foreseeable future. I reminded the ATO and his clerk where I was holed up, and went for a wander about the ship.

I knew I'd get lost pretty quickly, but it didn't matter as I had all day to find my way back. I spent time looking at the planes being repaired on the hangar deck, and went back to the jet shop in time to watch a jet engine being tested on the fantail. I picked up a copy of the ship's newspaper on the crew's mess deck. I'd seen it before; a few hundred copies were delivered to the *Harrisburg*, usually daily, with the mail. There was a short summary of international and national news; a television schedule, notices of training sessions, and a few short articles from the Safety Officer, the Medical Officer (shot notifications, and things not to eat while on leave), and a weather forecast.

I found the Public Affairs Office a short way down the passage from my stateroom. It shared a space with Educational Services, and a dubiously named Special Projects office.

It was a large compartment, roughly divided into three sections. The front part of the office was PAO. Five sailors of various ratings were at typewriters, while one desk, without a typewriter, was empty.

A Carly Simon album was playing on a record player on top of a filing cabinet. Movement was minimal on the 675-foot, 20,000-ton *Harrisburg*, but virtually non-existent on this 95,000-ton carrier, so using a record player wasn't a problem.

There were two junior officers at the desks towards the rear, each with a yeoman or two.

"Can I help you, sir?" one of the PAO men asked, looking up from his typewriter.

I introduced myself, and said I was PAO from the *Harrisburg*, temporarily stranded.

"Yeah, it's a mess," he said. I tried to read the name stencilled on his shirt, but it was too faded, and didn't look pronounceable anyway.

"The teletype signal isn't coming through, so we don't have any news for tomorrow's paper," he said.

"What do you do?" I asked.

"We have some syndicated stuff, and permission to reprint from *Time* and *Newsweek*," the sailor replied. "We're only supposed to use one article from each issue."

"Is your officer around?"

"Mr Grayson's on the bridge, sir. He's only been public affairs officer for about a week, so I am sure he'd like to talk to you about how things should be done. We've all told him, but he doesn't trust us."

The other men laughed at this.

"What's he doing on the bridge?" I asked.

"Well, sir, Mr Grayson has had about six jobs in the year he's been aboard, but if there's one thing he can do, he's about the best boat-driver on the ship. He's got the con, and will be trying to do an unrep about now."

An underway replenishment, whether fuel or cargo, was a dangerous operation at the best of times. Trying one in these conditions would normally not be undertaken, but aviation gasoline, or food must be urgently needed, either by the *Enterprise*, or whatever ship might come alongside to receive it.

"When he gets back to the office, please tell him I'm in Enterprise Plaza," I said.

"Yes, sir."

೮

Osgood had indulged me this digression, but I sensed I'd better get on with my story.

"What did Special Projects do?" he asked.

"When I met up with Grayson – nice guy, who treated me like a guru – he complained about sharing the space, as he could use two more desks. He said that Special Projects was headed by an Orion pilot with nothing to do except carry out the captain's latest *idée folle*."

"*Par example?*"

"The captain's girlfriend was aboard and saw a pin-up on the inside of a locker on the hangar deck," I related. "So, all lockers had to be purged of pin-ups. Special Projects was put in charge. The Special Projects yeoman told the guys in PAO, and between them, they spread word to the whole ship, so when the inspection was done, only one locker on the whole ship was found to have an offending poster. It belonged to a guy in Sick Bay with chicken pox. He was fined fifty dollars."

"Poor sod," Osgood said, laughing as hard as I had ever seen him do.

"Well, that story got around, and his shipmates felt so badly for him that they kept handing him five-dollar bills until he was well into profit."

"What else did Special Projects do?"

"We didn't discuss it that much, but I gather it was all about that level of sensitivity: arranging the Christmas tree for the hangar deck; organising a boxing match; that sort of thing."

"Continue."

∞

Having lost a day of air transfers, the ATO had me low on the priority list of helo flights. He was short a helo, as one had been unable to leave a destroyer once the gale had started, and hadn't yet returned. I told him that I'd been away from my ship for ten days.

"Well, another few hours isn't going to matter, then, is it?" he replied.

I couldn't argue with that.

It was dinnertime when I touched down on the *Harrisburg*, via two destroyers. I dumped my bag, and went to the mess, feeling relatively good to be back on board. Even the Admin officer feigned pleasure in seeing me when I gave him fifty typewriter ribbons.

After dinner, the executive officer told me that the captain wanted to see me.

"I told you you'd be back," he said, opening a file on his desk. "It seems I am to give you room and board, and arrange transport for you. I expect the government's still paying you, too."

"Yes, sir."

"My orders also say that in addition to providing hotel accommodation and flights to Saigon, I'm not to ask you what you're doing. It does not say that you cannot tell me," he said.

"No, sir," I replied as politely as I could. "Those were my orders."

"Ah."

"Well, f--- it. Try to make yourself useful, and stay out of the way. Dismissed."

I turned to leave, but he stopped me.

"When you get the chance, you can tell the Queen that you'll need alternative accommodation. The *Harrisburg*'s been ordered back to San Diego. We leave Yankee Station on November first. *And*, a new PAO is on his way."

That was only ten days away, and I had no way of contacting Hawthorne or the countess. As it turned out, I didn't have to wait long before I was summoned by the captain and handed a large brown envelope. He said nothing when he gave it to me, but made me sign a receipt.

I went to my office and opened the envelope. There was a simple typed sheet that said to go to the Hoàn-Mỹ at 1500 to hand over the enclosed envelope. Given my previous transport arrangements, I thought that was optimistic. I looked at the other envelope: it was a slightly smaller version of the outer one, and had "Top Secret" stamped twice on each side, and a security tape on the flap. I put it back in the larger envelope, put it in my document portfolio, and locked them in the desk safe in the VIP suite. As I did so, I thought I'd get a small brass plaque made saying "Statler Harrisburg" as a parting gesture, since the ship would be leaving without me.

At breakfast, the ATO told me there was a helo at 0900 to take me to the *America* for a flight to Tan Son Nyut.

The connection gods were with us: the helo transfer was twenty minutes, and the COD left twenty minutes after that. I started to believe that it wasn't just good luck when a staff sergeant met me at the terminal, holding a sign with my name on it. I left my bag at the BOQ, got in the jeep and headed into Saigon.

I was at the hotel in time for lunch, then crossed the street and walked along the river. It was about eighty degrees, but there was a breeze by the river, and I found a place to sit. I read my book, and watched the water traffic, and the spirals of planes waiting to land.

I returned to the hotel shortly before three, and sat near where I'd been with Hawthorne, and ordered a beer.

At about five minutes past three, a traditionally dressed Vietnamese woman came up to my table.

"Mr Bradley, I know a café near here," she said. "It will be better if we sit outside."

She turned and left the hotel. It happened so quickly that I couldn't guess her age, but was aware of her bright red lipstick and large, fashionable dark glasses. It also seemed that she was relatively tall, and her black hair fell to the bottom of her shoulder blades. Outside, she put on her conical *nón lá*, and walked up the street. She turned right and then into a small *cul-de-sac* where there were café tables. She chose a seat where she could watch the street entrance. We were in the shade of the building, and while she slipped the hat off her head again, she kept the dark glasses on.

"Our first meeting," she said. "Let's hope this is a profitable association for both of us."

A waiter came, and she ordered tea. She had the look of affluence about her: her hair was well cut; her nails were manicured; and her speech and movements refined. I also thought that her lips looked French; they had that Jeanne Moreau, Brigette Bardot fullness about them, emphasised by the too-red lipstick.

I had no doubt that she was eyeing me up in a similar way, wondering if I could be trusted, or if I was just another say-one-thing-do-another American. She had said nothing since we sat, but eyed my document case which was on the table.

When the waiter came with the tea things, I moved the portfolio to the chair next to me. She said a few words to him, which appeared to be another order. He nodded and left.

She poured the tea into the small cup, and passed it to me.

"They call you 'The Countess'," I said. "What would you like me to call you?"

She finished pouring her own tea, tasted it, and put the cup down carefully.

"You may call me whatever you want," she said.

Her English was excellent, with an accent, which I would find was a mix of French with the inflection of Vietnamese.

"That doesn't really help," I said. "You know my name; it's on my name badge. I expect you've been told my first name, too."

"Of course, I have, Bill," she said. "Or is that too familiar, Lieutenant? We have just met."

I was reminded of Myrna Loy as Fu Manchu's daughter.

"Did you meet Hawthorne?" I asked.

"I've met a great many people," she replied.

This conversation had long gaps between our sentences. I resolved to give as little away about myself as she did, but it did seem to be an unfriendly way of delivering broadcast scripts.

I was considering what to say next when the waiter returned with a plate stacked with small pancake rolls.

"They are called *chả giò*," the countess said. "They are like pancake rolls."

She picked one up in a paper napkin and began eating. I took a napkin, but picked up the roll in my fingers. It was still warm, and a good snack, and, after three months on Yankee Station, the first piece of Vietnamese food I'd had.

The waiter appeared again, this time with some fried round balls coated with sesame seeds.

"These are *bánh cam*," she said. "They are not particularly sweet, although they look like they will be."

Having finished the *chả giò*, I wiped my fingers and took a sesame ball. It was curiously soft. I watched the countess as she bit into one, while chewing, she turned the ball to me and I could see that it was hollow, but with another yellowish ball inside.

I bit mine, and as I chewed, the countess laughed.

"I will have to take you for a full dinner sometime," she said. "It will amuse me for hours."

I laughed.

"I know pancake rolls, but I've never tasted anything like this before," I said. "It's good, but unexpected."

She seemed to relax, but only a little. She asked what I'd seen of Saigon; how long I had been in the Navy, and where I was from. It was all very basic first conversation, but I kept my answers general.

"I was born here," she said. "My mother was French. I almost never see my father."

After those details, she said nothing more about herself, but asked what French writers I knew. Then painters, musicians, composers, and films. I asked what Americans she knew in the same categories. There was no doubt she was cultured, well-educated, and perceptive.

When we finished the snacks and the tea had gone cold, we sat for a few moments enjoying the shade and relative quiet of the café.

"I guess it's time for business," I said, reaching for my portfolio.

I undid the strap and withdrew the sealed envelope and handed it over.

"Thank you," she said, slipping it into the woven bag with a long shoulder strap that she wore.

She smiled for the second time.

"I hope this is the first of many meetings," she said, standing up.

"What is your name?" I asked again.

"I told you; you can call me whatever you like: Mary, Margaret, Patricia, Rachel, Andrea, Elisabeth, Simone, Valerie – you choose," she said, reeling off names like a litany. "Call me something different each time you see me; that would be fun."

She was almost teasing.

"You know, in Greek mythology, knowing someone's name gives you control over them," she said. "That is why I am only known as 'the countess'. *À bientôt.*"

As I reached for my file, the waiter appeared with the bill. I had neglected to ask Hawthorne about expenses. I paid the waiter, and walked back to the hotel to call for a ride back to Tan Son Nyut, as a C-130 roared overhead.

Chapter IV

"Of course, I never met the countess," Osgood said. "That was all handled in Hawthorne's time. How did you feel about your first encounter with her?"

"Out of my depth. I realised I'd never played hardball," I said. "On the way back to the ship, I replayed our meeting. I decided that I talked too much, from nervousness. But, I didn't give anything useful away."

If I wanted reassurance, Osgood wasn't going to give it to me.

"Who recruited her?" I asked.

Osgood shrugged and opened his hands.

"Hawthorne, probably."

I didn't believe this vagueness. I knew he wouldn't tell me until it suited him, so I didn't ask. After twenty years of working with Osgood, I didn't know him well, but well enough.

"I thought it was the Americans who engaged her," I said.

"What gave you that idea?" Osgood asked, seemingly surprised."

"Well, Hawthorne, and then the countess," I said.

"She told you that? When?"

He sat up, and leaned forward.

"I haven't got to that part yet," I said.

Osgood made one of his hand gestures, the one that signalled impatience.

"Well, get to it soon. Anyway, it was Hawthorne's show," he said. "He may have found some American to talk to the countess. It's not really important."

Wasn't it?

He refocussed.

"How did you feel about the countess herself?"

"Ambivalent," I said. "There was something thrilling about having an assignation with a beautiful, mysterious agent in a dangerous city. I'd seen all the spy films, and I was a perfect parody, though I never sensed I was being mocked.

"It was frustrating not being able to see her eyes; get a hint of what she was thinking. I wanted to know how many times she'd done this before. You've seen my journal entries, you know my first reactions. After several months on a ship, female company was welcome, if only for some tea and mung bean cakes."

"Did you ever doubt that she was the countess?" he asked.

"No. I'd been in the Majestic before and no one had approached me by name. We had no code to identify ourselves."

"What did you make of that, if you'd seen all the spy films?" Osgood asked.

He hadn't asked me this question in previous debriefings or reviews.

"It puzzled me at first, but then I thought that this was a dry run, with dummy papers that wouldn't cause problems if they fell into the wrong hands," I said.

Osgood nodded, and I thought there was a hint of a smile.

"Tell me the next stage."

§

I had made no arrangement to get back to Tan Son Nhut, and went back to the Majestic to call the motor pool. As I approached the entrance, I saw the jeep and driver who had brought me, and we headed back. At the terminal, I was told that there was a flight to the *Midway,* in an hour. I went to the BOQ to collect my bag and was on my way. The ATO on the *Midway* put me on a helo within half an hour of landing, and although we stopped at three other ships *en route*, I was back on the *Harrisburg* before 2100.

I wasn't hungry, but stopped in the office to see if anything urgent had come in.

Lieutenant Briggs, the Admin officer, gave me his usual taciturn greeting when I walked in.

"How was your little junket? Get in a round of golf?" he asked.

"Only six over, today," I said, opening my copy of *All Hands* and sitting down to read.

"The XO told me that the new PAO would be arriving next week," Briggs said.

"Yes, the captain told me yesterday," I said. "I'm waiting to see where I get transferred to next. I hope it's not the Tan Son Nhut BOQ. I've already spent too much time there."

"Best to stay with the Navy," Briggs agreed. "At least most of us are normal."

There was more to that than I suspected. Briggs went on to tell me how he'd spent a week stranded with the Air Force on the way to his first tour of Vietnam.

"Black-shoes and brown-shoes seldom mix, or understand each other, so what chance is there to grasp what the air farce guys are talking about?" he said.

He paused a moment.

"I know they've got you doing something spooky; it can't

be anything else," he said quietly. "Be careful; they're all treacherous."

"Thanks," I said, for this unexpected concern. "You must be looking forward to getting stateside."

We drained the coffee pot and talked until nearly midnight. It's easy to be nice to someone who's leaving imminently.

The next morning, I wrote up my first meeting with the countess in the office, then went to my stateroom and locked it in the safe.

Later that morning, my yeoman gave me a press release to review. He'd learned a lot, so there wasn't much to fix, and I spent the rest of the morning taking pictures around the ship for the annual cruise book. At present, the book consisted only of a large box of blank pages, crew and squadron lists, and photographs of varying quality. Putting it together would be a nightmare for whoever got the job.

Public Affairs also was normally delegated with the task of writing the command history, too. It was one of the ship's secretary's jobs that he usually off-loaded to some junior officer.

Two days later, after lunch, the XO told me that the captain wanted to see me. This would either be my orders off the *Harrisburg*, or afternoon tea with the countess.

"Mr Bradley, I appear to be your messenger," the captain said. "This may be the last time."

He handed me the normal order papers.

"Collect your service jacket in the normal way, and commence check out tomorrow," he said.

The orders were fairly simple: in two days I was to report to the *USS Hartford*, another World War II era cruiser. In the comments section of the orders was written, "Accommodation Only."

Like all things in the military, transferring from one assignment to the next is a complex business where everything happens at once. There were mess bills to be settled, pay-to-date to be collected, duties to be handed over (very few in my case), and all one's possessions to be tracked down and packed. The ATO told me I'd be on an 0800 helo.

I didn't know where the *Hartford* was; I didn't know within a few hundred miles, where the *Harrisburg* was. That was a curious thing about being on a ship: if your job didn't actually involve knowing where you were, it didn't matter, and you could go for weeks, months even, without any idea where you were or, what direction you were headed. Even on the bridge as the OOD, which had fallen to me as a matter of course, I didn't know where we were, only what course we were on, and how long we were supposed to hold it.

On my last night aboard, I was doing some last things at my desk, when at about ten o'clock, Briggs came up to me.

"Take a break for a few minutes," he said. "I want to show you something."

I followed him around the bookcase that separated PAO from Admin, and found six of my fellow junior officers sitting around the central table, and a fifth of Johnny Walker in the middle.

ೞ

The flight to the *Hartford* took nearly an hour. The weather was clear, but I wasn't near a window, and only had a brief warning before we set down.

The *Hartford* was more than a hundred feet shorter than the *Harrisburg*. A 1945 Cleveland Class light cruiser, its complement in normal times was more than 1,250, but the cuts already in place had trimmed the actual crew to just under 1,100. Like the *Harrisburg*, the *Hartford* had been converted to a guided missile cruiser, and had lost usable space throughout the ship.

I went through the normal check in procedure, was given a stateroom with another j.g. It was a stateroom for four, but there would only be two of us in it.

I was unpacking when my roommate came in.

"I'm afraid I've invaded your private stateroom," I said, and introduced myself.

"Gordon Russo, damage control," he said, extending his hand.

"I guess you don't see much daylight," I said.

"Is it winter or summer?" he laughed. "I'm just going for some lunch. I'll take you to the wardroom."

Though smaller, the wardroom was much as the one on the *Harrisburg* with five long tables, each seating about twenty. The food was better.

"I hear on destroyers they even cook the men's eggs to order," one of the junior officers near me said.

Then, one of them asked the dreaded question.

"What will you be doing aboard the *Hartford*?"

I had a few answers to this, but they sounded somewhere between pompous and flippant.

"I'm on a special assignment," I said as casually as I could.

They immediately looked wary.

"I can tell you that I'm not doing an investigation; I'm not looking for drink, drugs or – "

"Women!" an ensign blurted.

"Speak for yourself," I replied, while everyone was still

afraid to laugh.

The noise that followed earned us impatient looks from further up the table where more senior officers sat.

Lunch was less formal than dinner, and everyone else had jobs to get back to. As I left the wardroom, I had it in mind to find the public affairs officer and see if I could be of any use, but a lieutenant intercepted me.

"Mr Bradley," he said. "The XO sends his compliments, and would you let me take you to his office."

This wasn't a typical Navy exchange, which would have been more like, "Mr Bradley, report to the XO." Everyone on a ship knows that XOs have to be tough; some enjoy it more than others. They are also your strongest allies if they believe in you. I'd not experienced it, but had seen it several times.

We passed through the outer office, and my escort knocked on the XO's door, opened it, announced me, and closed the door, leaving me alone with the XO.

Commander Keyser was not a big man, but was no less imposing. He had thick black eyebrows like a member of the Politburo, broad shoulders, and an intimidating stare. I could imagine guilty sailors spilling their guts after about ninety seconds, and junior officers losing their lunch equally quickly.

I don't know what I thought he was going to do when he stood up, but he extended his hand, and gave an engaging smile.

"Welcome aboard, Mr Bradley," he said.

The smile disappeared as he sat down, and told me to do the same. He had my service record in front of him, and read through it again for a few seconds.

"The *Harrisburg* was your first assignment afloat?"

"Yes, XO."

"How big was public affairs?"

I told him about our feeble strength.

"And you did time as ATO, too."

"Yes, sir."

"How did you get on with that?"

"I only did it for a few weeks, sir. I felt I was just getting handle on it when I was moved back to PAO," I said.

He closed my file and gave a sigh. I couldn't tell for sure what type of sigh it was; one resigned to the way things were?

"How did you get involved in this curious TAD assignment?" he asked, fixing me with his stare.

I told him about the typewriter ribbons, the chance meeting with Hawthorne, my subsequent time at Tan Son

Nhut, and the formalisation of the temporary duty.

Throughout my narrative, he seemed not to move, even blink.

"How often do you expect to be ordered to Saigon?"

"I was told about once a week, sir."

He continued his fixed position, then sat back in his chair and put his fingers together.

"Here's the thing: we're not running a hotel. I can't tell from your orders what your chain of command is. It just says temporarily assigned to the Ministry of Defence of the United Kingdom."

He thought some more.

"Let me ask you this: how do you propose to spend your time on board? Presumably when you're not in Saigon, you have some work to be done?"

"I write up the content of our meetings, sir."

I did not add that these notes were for me, and that I had not been asked by Hawthorne to do any more than hand-over an envelope.

"So, I repeat: how do you propose to spend your time aboard the *Hartford*?"

"As long as I am able to depart when ordered without delay, I'll do as ordered, sir," I said. "I was going to visit the public affairs office to see if I could be useful, before I was requested to see you."

"You stood bridge watches on the *Harrisburg*. What kind of boat-driver are you?"

"Adequate, sir."

He looked up from his desk.

"Your captain rated you higher than that," he said.

I had not seen my separation fitness report.

"Very well. Visit Mr Bassett in PAO, then tomorrow, report to the bridge with the OOD for the 0800 watch. You can shadow him to see how we do things on the *Hartford*."

I was about to reply when he said:

"Dismissed."

"Thank you, sir."

૮૦

I was in the wardroom at 0630 the next morning when the lieutenant, who appeared to be the XO's assistant, told me to see the XO before 0700.

That could only mean one thing: a message for the countess.

Chapter V

"It seems that you will escape bridge watch today, Mr Bradley," the XO said. "Here are your orders. Your helo leaves at 0730."

No pleasantries today.

The helo arrived on schedule, and after a few stops, landed on the *USS Saratoga*. I had two hours before the scheduled COD departure, so went to the wardroom for some coffee. I had only had a cursory glance at my instructions, noting that my appointment was at 1430. This time, the address was a café, not the one where we had our first meeting.

These trips gave me much time to think about what I was doing and why. Surely there were easier, less personal ways of delivering propaganda, unless what I was delivering weren't radio scripts.

The rest of the journey went as before. I was met by Staff Sergeant Borroughs who drove me to the café. It was typical French colonial, on a busy street opposite the wooded Mạc Đĩnh Chi Cemetery.

"That's where all the important French are buried," Borroughs said. "We're a few minutes early, sir, so I'll drive around the park and show you where I'll be waiting."

On the opposite side to the café, a number of jeeps and staff cars were parked.

"I'll be there, sir."

"Will you be able to do something with your time?" I asked.

"I can get lunch, sir," he said. "I've been driving since 0800."

Borroughs drove me back to the café where I took a seat against the wall of the building, out of the sun, and with a view of the street and cemetery. I ordered a beer when the waiter came. Was I drinking on duty? I wondered, but didn't see how anyone except MI7 could complain, and the British attitude to alcohol was considerably different to that of the American military.

The countess arrived just as the waiter was serving my beer. She placed an order in French.

"You should drink something traditional," she said, sitting down.

"What did you order" I asked.

"Dry white wine."

"They still have it?" I asked, not imagining that wine shipments to Saigon had been very frequent since Dien Bien Phu.

"There isn't much, but what's left is very good," she said, smiling.

She looked exactly as before. Same red lips and fingernails, white *áo dài*, palm leaf hat, and dark glasses. She slipped her hat off and let it hang down her back. She had a woven grass shopping bag, open at the top, but I couldn't see what was inside.

"One day, we'll have dinner and you can try some very good red wine," she continued. "The selection isn't what it was, but there's still a lot of claret around in the café cellars."

Her drink came.

"*Santé*," she said, and I raised my beer.

"How is your new ship?" she asked.

"I only joined it last night," I said, surprised that she knew.

"Well, I hope the food is good, and that you're comfortable," she said.

"Have you been doing this long?" I asked.

With her dark glasses, it was impossible to tell what she was thinking.

"Acting as a courier? A while."

"Who did you work with before?" I asked.

"Another sailor," she replied.

"Was he discharged?"

"No, they had him killed. Would you like some olives or nuts?"

I guessed that the countess was little older than I was. She was inscrutable talking about my predecessor, and I wondered if she'd talk about my fate with the same lack of interest.

"For delivering propaganda scripts?" I asked, suddenly more concerned about my future than I had been since meeting Hawthorne.

"I do not know why they killed him," she said. "I didn't think he was very nice."

"Apparently, someone else agreed with you."

She waved to the waiter and ordered nuts and olives.

"Would you like another beer?"

I nodded, and she asked for another white wine.

"Were you recruited by Hawthorne?" I asked.

"Is he the one who engaged you?"

"Yes."

"You were engaged by the British. I was engaged by the Americans; a nice man. A Navy commander. He's dead, too. We don't know the same people," she explained, then added: "I don't know who recruited my other contacts."

"You pass on the information?"

"We shouldn't talk about these things. It's not safe."

"Is that why your last contact was killed?" I asked.

"I don't know," she said. "It might have been something else entirely; he might have had gambling debts; they're not very forgiving here. People go back to the USA very quickly, and debts aren't paid. Maybe he ran up too many bar bills; or hurt one of the girls. There are lots of reasons to be killed here."

I waited to see if she'd say more.

"You were given an envelope; you opened it, and inside were instructions for you. Inside the envelope you hand over are instructions for me," she said. "Sometimes, there is another envelope for me to hand to someone else. Sometimes, it's something for me to do."

The olives and nuts arrived along with our drinks.

"It's like a Russian doll," she said. "It's not a good idea to know what is in the final one."

She said this darkly, and it added to the uncertainty I had

65

on the transport plane, wondering if this was merely propaganda.

"Why do I need to live on a ship and fly here?" I asked.

She looked at me patiently.

"That is something you will have to work out," she said. "But I will give you a hint: think of the alternatives."

We ate our olives, nibbled our nuts, and enjoyed our drinks. The countess chatted, telling me about how shopping could become difficult because of interrupted supplies from the country.

"Prices can change during the day for meat, vegetables, rice, and noodles," she explained. "It's better if you have dollars to pay with. There are some places that won't accept them, and other places still accept francs, but they are rare."

I mentioned that I'd wondered about expenses, but that I had no way of contacting Hawthorne.

"I can't contact the people who hired me, either," she said. "You're being paid though, like me. Maybe your bank details haven't caught up with you yet."

Hawthorne had mentioned a UK account, but that wouldn't do me any good for a long time – which was probably the point.

"What will you do on your new ship?" the countess asked.

"I don't know. I was supposed to be on the bridge this morning learning from the OOD, but my trip here stopped that."

"OOD?"

"Officer of the deck. The one who drives the boat," I said.

"You turn the wheel?"

"No. The OOD gives orders to a quartermaster who turns the wheel," I said, realising how complicated this was to anyone who didn't know anything about how the Navy worked.

"But, you still say that you are the one driving," there was an ironic smile.

"Like wine growers who talk about making wine, but never touch a grape."

"*That*, I understand," she laughed.

"Are you from Saigon?" I asked, knowing I was entering dangerous ground.

She took the question as casual chat.

"I grew up *au faubourg*, in what you'd call the suburbs, in Thao Dien," she said. "District two; do you know the districts yet? A lot of French lived there, as it was thought to be safer than being in the middle of Saigon. It's about fifteen minutes from here."

She wanted to know about where I came from, so I told her about the joys of Centerburg, Ohio, and its tiny population.

As the olives, nuts and drinks were gone, it was time to hand over my envelope, and make my way back to the ship.

"Thank you, Lieutenant Bradley," she said.

She reached down and picked up her grass bag and handed it to me.

"What's this?" I said looking in the bag.

"A few things your office will thank you for," she said. "Wherever you'll be working."

"Thank you, Countess."

"À bientôt."

I walked around the square, to where Sergeant Borroughs said he'd wait. I found the Jeep and climbed in. I had a look in the bag and found a handful of 45s: The Isley Brothers, "Work to Do"; Gilbert O'Sullivan's "Clair"; "Dancing in the Moonlight," by King Harvest; and "Corner of the Sky," by the Jackson 5. These records had just been released. I'd heard them in the last few days on the *Harrisburg* on the unreliable AFRTS from Saigon, but no one on the ship would have copies. The other things in the bag were IBM typewriter ribbons.

ଔ

"The songs were very thoughtful, but the ribbons were pure Hawthorne," I said to Osgood.

"You learned nothing about her except where she used to live," he said.

"I didn't realise I was supposed to be gathering intelligence," I replied, slightly resenting the implication that I hadn't done my job. "I wanted to learn more about her; who she was; what she did; did she work? Have a boyfriend; anything."

"What was stopping you?"

"Two things, I think. First, these early meetings were pleasant encounters; congenial, if not yet relaxed. There was something exceptional about sitting in a French café, drinking with a pretty, mysterious girl in the middle of a war zone."

"And second?"

"I couldn't see her eyes," I said. "I didn't want to get onto topics where honesty was important without being able to judge the veracity by seeing her eyes."

"You said she was inscrutable."

"Yes. Today, that would be called racial stereotyping."

"Stereotypes didn't come from nowhere," Osgood said.

"Given the context of Southeast Asia, I thought it was a

fair observation," I said.

"You said, 'topics where honesty was important,'" Osgood said. "What did you mean by that?"

"Just those personal things I mentioned," I replied. "I didn't think I could, or should, ask anything further about what was in her envelopes; how she was recruited; or what sort of things she was asked to do, other than hand over papers. One thing I thought I could eventually ask was about her parents; what they did; and, if they were still around."

"What were the reasons you felt you couldn't ask about her work for us?"

"When you're on shipboard and visiting foreign countries, it's made very clear to everyone that you should be very careful about what you say about the ship's operations," I said. "This is more critical in a war zone. I didn't know if the countess was a volunteer, or doing whatever she did under duress.

"I also thought that if I pried, she wouldn't tell me anything, and our meetings would be very short and formal."

"Did you have any sense of how long these meetings would go on?" Osgood asked.

"I knew the peace talks were underway, although the reports said they were stalled. I certainly had no idea what was coming next."

"When did you work out why it was important for you to be on the ship?"

"The trouble and expense of transporting me around by helo, COD and Jeep must have been enormous, and I couldn't see that anyone was getting any value from it," I began. "The countess gave me the clue, though: what would be the alternative? Even I worked that one out fairly quickly: the alternative would be to live in Saigon, and be suspected of being a spy. An unattached American, in or out of uniform, living in Saigon, would pretty quickly be suspected of something covert. Living at the air base wouldn't be much better. ARVN officers and men weren't fully trusted; indeed, I sensed in my limited time there that the trust was declining at a time when it should have been greatest."

Osgood nodded.

"Very well. What happened next?"

Chapter VI

The new records and typewriter ribbons bought me a friendly welcome in the public affairs office. It was run by Ensign Paul Gumerie, who was able, but having to find his own way. He was assisted by a second class petty officer and a seaman who had things pretty much under control.

"The XO told me that Mr Bassett ran PAO," I said.

He laughed, and shook his head.

"Bassett left two years ago," Ensign Gumerie said. "No one here ever knew him."

In addition to its normal functions, PAO also operated the ship's radio station (WHAR) and was able to broadcast 16mm films to the *Hartford's* closed-circuit televisions. Most of the radio was canned AFRTS long-playing records which arrived in heavy boxes each week.

Live radio was provided by the WHAR station manager, a talented seaman, who did the news and weather three times a day. A succession of music broadcasts from pop, country and western, Motown, rhythm and blues, and jazz, were presented by volunteers of varying abilities.

The XO made sure I observed a bridge watch before putting me on the rota, and Paul Gumerie handed me the cruise book to get underway. This gave me flexibility, as I spent much of the time walking around the ship taking pictures at different times of the day, and of the fullest range of activities that I could. I also met with the ship's photo department to make a schedule for all the departments and divisions to be photographed.

The days went by, and soon it was December; three weeks without instructions to see the countess. I stayed out of the XO's way, but I wondered about the hiatus.

There's a curious phenomenon on a ship – I don't know if it's true at other than military facilities – but it is possible to sense events building, even though you are not involved, and know nothing about them. It might start with taking on extra supplies and more fuel fairly shortly after the last replenishment; it might be a casual remark by one of the guys working in communications that there's been a lot of traffic; or, it might be the news that one or more carriers has arrived on Yankee Station, and none has left.

In the early weeks of December, all of these things were happening, as I carried out my normal watches and daily routine as auxiliary PAO. I even mentioned this confluence of circumstances to Ensign Gumerie, and suggested that it would not surprise me to receive orders in the next day or so.

I was taken off guard, as when in the morning there were no orders to see the countess, I thought that was it for the day. I was entering the wardroom for lunch when the XO's assistant intercepted me.

"The XO would like to see you, Mr Bradley," he said, shortly.

Half an hour later, I was on the helo pad with an overnight bag and my latest delivery for the countess. We were to meet at another café, but not until 1730. Chances of my return before the next day were remote.

Sergeant Borroughs met me, and said he knew the café in question. I dropped off my bag at the BOQ, and asked the duty clerk to hold a room for me.

"Good idea, sir," the corporal said. "We're pretty full tonight."

It was another piece of supporting evidence to the theory.

With only my document portfolio, I went out to the Jeep.

"All set, sir?" Sergeant Borroughs asked.

He was a pleasant twenty-one-year-old from Idaho. He never asked questions beyond, "How are you?" or "Did you have a good flight?", though I am sure he had seen me with the countess.

When you're thinking about something, you are much more aware of anything related to it, so the number of planes flying in and out of Tan Son Nhut seemed higher to me that day, but it may just have been an illusion.

I wasn't certain where, or if, any of this was related to what the countess and I were doing, but I had a pretty good idea.

That feeling was confirmed when Sergeant Borroughs dropped me at the café, and I saw the countess already there with a pot of tea in front of her.

"I'm not late, am I?" I said, as I sat down.

She shook her head.

"The guys in public affairs send their thanks for the records and the ribbons," I said.

"They deserve a few rewards."

She hadn't smiled, and her manner was subdued. She was dressed in a similar way, but today her *áo dài* was light brown. Her hat was off; her make-up and nails, the same.

"Where are we?" I asked.

"About a mile from where we were the last time," she said. "The river is that way, only a few hundred yards."

She stopped halfway through her answer to wait for the noise of a plane to pass.

"How long has it been this noisy?" I asked.

"It started on the weekend," she said.

I didn't ask her if she knew what was going on.

"Can you stay for dinner?" she asked.

"When?"

"In about an hour," she said. "It's early, but I want to get home. Don't order lots of food with your tea."

The waiter was there in a moment, and I only ordered tea.

"Do you know what's happening?" she asked.

I shook my head.

"I can only guess," I said. "The talks aren't going well, so a little persuasion is in order."

"Basic Machiavelli," she said. "I hope it's just to remind them. No one here knows what a normal life is."

"Do you have enough food?" I asked.

She smiled at my question, and looked lovely.

"Dear Lieutenant Bradley; yes, I do," she replied. "I have bags of rice; cans of vegetables, and some meat; I have rice flour; I have oil. There are vegetables grown in the neighbourhood. If it gets bad, it will be sealed off so those who live there can eat."

"If I can bring you anything from the ship . . . ."

"I will let you know," she said softly.

She asked me what I was reading. I had recently traded a few books for one about the films of François Truffaut. I hadn't *seen* many of them, but hoped I could bluff it.

"*La Sirene du Mississippi* is my favourite of the recent films," she said. "Have you seen it?"

"No," I admitted, "but I liked *Fahrenheit 451* very much."

"But it was so cold, stark," she said. "None of the characters have any warmth."

"No, they don't. I think that's the point," I said. "They are the faceless, flat product of a faceless flat time. What's important are the printed words; those letters moving across the screen with all the form and detail of the type, saying something against the stark, featureless background."

She helped herself to hot tea from my pot.

"That's good," she said, thinking. "It makes sense of the other things."

"The book-burning scenes are strong; watching the words disappear into ashes; it makes you realise how precious those things are."

"What about *La Mariée était en noir*?" the countess asked.

"Wonderful music," I said. "Some good images, but no suspense: you know what she's going to do, then you watch her do it. Seeing Julie get vengeance is satisfying, but there's little drama."

"Can you not imagine how she feels? Her happiest moment instantly turned to her most tragic?"

I looked at her.

"Countess, are you a romantic? I never would have guessed!"

She smiled, and I almost thought she blushed.

"I think there are a lot of things about me that you'd never guess," she said very softly.

I suspected I'd get nothing further from her, so reached for the portfolio and started to hand it over.

"Are you leaving? Will you go back to the ship tonight?" she asked, with the hint of disappointment in her voice.

"I've reserved a room at the BOQ," I said.

"Then, stay here for something to eat. The food will be better than at the officers' club."

I sat down again, and she signalled for the waiter. My French was just good enough to understand that she asked for a place for dinner, and we moved to a square table against the front of the building, further back from the street. It was laid with a cloth, cutlery and wine glasses. We were given menus as we were seated.

It was in Vietnamese, French, and amusing English. I was looking down the list which was pretty eclectic, when I realised the countess had slid her dark glasses up onto her head. I dropped the menu onto the table, and she looked up to see me staring at her.

"Is something wrong?" she asked.

I blinked and continued to stare.

"I've never seen you without your dark glasses."

"I can't see to read in this shade; they're too dark," she said. "You look surprised."

I looked into her pale blue eyes before replying.

"I had no idea you were Caucasian," I exclaimed. "You said your mother was French . . . ."

She visibly relaxed and laughed.

". . . you never said what your father was."

"He was British," she said, easily.

"Hence, the liaison work."

"Hence, the liaison work," she repeated, nodding.

"And here was me thinking you were inscrutable."

"I try to be. That's why I dress like a native," she said. "It's also practical, cool, and comfortable, and if you soak the leaf hats in water, the evaporation is very cooling."

"The bright red lipstick keeps people from looking at your

eyes," I said.

"And a few make-up tricks, but there's no hiding blue eyes," she said with mock coyness.

"And your hair?" I asked.

"It's a different colour," she admitted. "I take off my glasses, and get a flood of personal questions. You see why I maintain the disguise."

It was my turn to laugh, and apologise.

"I am very glad to see you relax, Lieutenant. Conversations were getting to be like tea with the ambassador," she said.

"Is the wine here drinkable?" I asked.

"It's all right. It won't be what it says on the label, so just get the cheap one; they're all the same. Probably made in Nha Trang from a blend of grapes and plums," she said.

"What else do you recommend?"

"Anything Vietnamese."

"You'll have to order for me."

∞

"Was that the beginning of a beautiful friendship?" Osgood asked.

"It might have been," I said. "It was easier to relate to her, but whatever our business was, it was important to maintain the distance when in public – which we always were."

"Were you afraid of anything in particular?"

"While we explored those things we had in common, and those we did not, I still didn't know her; and still didn't know how much I could trust her. Though I did let her order dinner."

"The irony wasn't lost on me," Osgood said. "You didn't say what you were afraid of."

"Being careless," I replied. "I didn't know what I was really doing; I had no training as a spy, and didn't consider myself one. I did know that if Borroughs, for example, saw me drinking, laughing, and holding hands with a lovely lady while he was waiting hours for me in the baking heat, then that news would be all over Tan Son Nhut before I got up in the morning. And, by then, I'd met a few dozen people who would recognise me. At least Borroughs knew I was doing something vaguely official."

"Did you tell the countess that?"

"Yes."

"What did she say?" Osgood asked.

"She said she had a reputation to protect, too, and we both laughed about it until the waiter came, and asked what we wanted to eat."

"Apart from the fact that she had blue eyes, did you learn anything?" Osgood asked, becoming serious.

"Her mother was from a French colonial family, born in Vietnam to a Parisian mother and a government official from Bordeaux. They both survived the withdrawal of the French, and he was kept on as a bureaucrat, eventually earning the respect of the new regime. Her mother and grand-parents are buried in Mạc Đinh Chi, the cemetery by the café we'd met in," I said.

"Were buried there," Osgood corrected. "After the fall of Saigon, families were given a few months to move the bodies. It's a public park now."

I didn't know this, and wondered if the countess did.

"Her father, she described as an adventurer," I continued. "He was British but born in India or Hong Kong, as I mentioned. He acquired an appetite for risk in World War II, and continued doing risky jobs; making deliveries; selling arms; fighting as a mercenary in Africa.

"The countess speaks very warmly of him. Even though he wasn't around much, he was good to both her and her mother, and brought money when he came, which was about twice a year," I related. "Money doesn't appear to have been a problem."

"No, it doesn't," Osgood agreed. "That was one of the reasons the ministry thought she might make a good agent.

Also, we thought she might have had some dreams or fantasies about having a glamorous, action-filled life like her father. Perhaps to impress him, but I'm not sure she felt that need."

"For action, or to impress?"

"To impress. From what we can tell, and you have previously said, they were close, and he seemed to adore her."

"I think he adored her mother, too," I said. "She appears to have accepted him as he was."

"What else happened that evening?" Osgood asked, moving back to business.

"We ate; I handed over the papers, and said good-night," I said. "We told each other to be careful, and I went to find Burroughs. It was still before eight o'clock, because I was back at the BOQ by eight-thirty.

"After breakfast, I went to the terminal, and was back on the *Hartford* by noon."

"That date was?"

"December tenth," I said. "After writing my journal, I wrote Christmas cards."

"Tell me about the next meeting."

"No, wait!" I said suddenly. "The countess said she was recruited by the Americans. You suggested she was recruited by Hawthorne."

"By Hawthorne, or on his instructions; does it matter?" Osgood said, letting a *soupçon* of uncharacteristic irritation show. "We were all on the same side. More or less."

Chapter VII

At 0630 on the morning of December 18, the XO's lieutenant, whose name, by his new name badge, I could now see was Griffith, knocked on my stateroom door, and told me to be ready for an 0700 helo, and to collect orders from the XO in his office.

After what the countess and I had said about a build-up, this meeting was not unexpected, and I was ready to go. I put two paperbacks in my portfolio, and went to collect my orders from the XO.

"I don't like running errands for junior officers," the commander said, handing over the envelope.

"I'm sorry, sir. Maybe one day I'll have more rank."

It was early, and I hadn't had time to secure my mouth. Judging by his look, I thought I'd be gigged on the spot, but after about ten seconds of his stare, he burst into a short laugh.

"Get out of here, mister!" he shouted.

The ATO was nearing the end of what had been a busy shift, and not apt to be open to marginal remarks.

"I've got one seat," he said to me as we walked towards the helo. "I had to bounce a lieutenant commander to get you on, and he was not happy. Good luck."

He'd never wished me luck before, and it was another one of those small indicators.

The *Midway* was launching aircraft when we approached, and we hovered on the starboard side so as not to be in the way of the rescue helicopter that always stood by when carriers were launching or recovering.

It was nearly half an hour before we could touch down. The *Midway*'s ATO, although at the start of his watch, was already frazzled.

"I hope you've got something to do," he said. "I don't see how I can get you off before 1630. As you can see, it's intensive air ops today, and the COD isn't due to land until 1500. Chances are, the crew won't have had lunch. I see I can bump anything up to a lieutenant commander to get you aboard, but sometimes it's not worth the hassle."

"I know what you're saying, Lieutenant," I said. "If there's a problem, call the XO."

"Okay, Bradley," he said. "I guess there's a reason you have priority over a lieutenant commander."

"I'll be in the wardroom."

The stewards gave me the breakfast I had missed. Afterwards, I read my orders. I was to meet the countess at 1400 at yet another café. I had time to check a map of Saigon that I pinched from the *Hartford*'s library. It wasn't near anywhere we'd been before, and it didn't look like I'd get there this time.

I had no way of alerting the countess, and could only hope that her contact had some way of letting her know of the change of plans. I knew that Commander Keyser would know where I was until my flight off the *Midway*, and hoped new orders would catch up with me.

To break the monotony, I walked up to the hangar deck. The ordnance crews were busy collecting trolleys full of bombs from the magazine elevators and arming them prior to being sent to the flight deck. Judging by the number of bombs on the hangar deck, there were going to be plenty more sorties today.

I went to a sponson on the port side and saw the rescue helo take up position for recovery. I climbed into the island and found a hatch to one of the viewing galleries, known as vultures' row. Planes were making the long arc to begin landing. It was 1140.

As I watched the carefully choreographed movements of the air crews as they prepared for recovery, I was calculating where this strike might have been. As the first few planes slammed on the deck, pulling the screaming arresting cable out, it came to me.

All the pieces were starting to fit, from the stalled peace talks, the extra comms traffic on the *Hartford*, the increased activity at my last visit to Tan Son Nhut, and today's bomb-laden sorties: these planes had been bombing Hanoi.

∞

After watching the recovery, I went down to lunch and sat with some ship's company junior officers. About halfway through my meal, the ATO joined me.

"We appear to still be on schedule," Lieutenant Chrobak said. "Come up at 1600 and I'll have a better idea then."

"How did the Hanoi bombing go?" I asked. "All birds back safely?"

He looked at me with some surprise, but ignored the first question.

"Everyone back safe," he said. "One had a bomb that hadn't dropped, and flew around the ship trying to shake it before needing to land. The risk is that hitting the deck and the sudden stop drops it on the deck."

"I gather that didn't happen."

"The AOs are incredible," he said. "They just rushed out to fix it, without hesitation. The release mechanism will be fully checked out before the next mission."

We had the usual informal conversation, not giving much away, but laying the groundwork for what could be a useful acquaintance. While this sounds calculated, it was the best that could be done in such circumstances, and paths re-cross in curious ways in the military.

After lunch, I went back to vultures' row. Planes were being re-spotted, but there were no launches or recoveries. A sailor who came out for some fresh air told me that a launch had taken place while I was having lunch. If launching had started at 1315, I wouldn't expect recovery operations to start until about 1545, making a 1630 COD flight unlikely.

While the sailor had been with me for less than ten minutes, we had been observed from the bridge, as vulture's row could easily be seen. A commander came out, and watched the passing scene with me for a few moments before speaking.

"Do you have some place to be, Lieutenant?" he asked.

While not overtly hostile, his tone was, "Don't mess with me," which never brought out my best.

"Yes, Commander," I said. "I should have been in Saigon for a 1400 appointment."

He considered this.

"Well, don't you have duties you could be getting on with?" he asked, with less patience in his voice than before.

"No, sir. Getting to Saigon is my duty, sir."

"Are you part of *Midway*'s ship's company?" he asked.

"I'm embarked on the *Hartford*, sir."

"And what do you do on the *Hartford*?" he asked, with rising sarcasm.

"I'm TAD with the British Ministry of Defence, Commander."

"And I bet you're just dying to tell me that you can't tell me what you're doing for them," he said.

It was one of those non-questions that demanded an answer.

"Your second assumption is correct, sir," I said.

He thought a moment to remember what he'd said.

"Very well, Lieutenant, but I suggest you confine yourself to the wardroom, or the ATO's office."

"Yes, sir."

There was no way I was going to thank him for his suggestion.

At around 1530, I could hear and feel the planes returning, and shortly after 1600, the wardroom began filling up with officers with 0800-1600 responsibilities. Not long after that, an ensign saw me sitting on my own, reading, and approached.

"Mr Bradley?" he asked, tentatively.

"Yes."

"There's a sailor in the passage to take you to the flight deck," he said. "He says your COD is ready."

I laughed.

"It's not just mine, Ensign."

I was airborne at 1640. It was about an hour and forty minutes to Tan Son Nhut, and the faithful Sergeant Borroughs was waiting for me in the terminal.

"Long day, Mr Bradley," he said, cheerfully. "I've taken the liberty of reserving you a room at the BOQ, and the personnel officer has new orders for you."

"Let's go there first," I said.

Sergeant Borroughs took my overnight bag, and led me to the personnel office where I signed for the new envelope. Opening it, there was a new time and address.

"What time do you think we should leave to get there by 1000?" I asked.

"I'll be at the BOQ at 0915, sir," he said.

"Thank you, Sergeant. I can find my way to the BOQ from

here," I said, as we started in different directions. "Wait a moment, Sergeant."

He turned back to me.

"Here," I said, taking two paperbacks from my portfolio, and giving them to him. "I've seen you reading in the Jeep."

"*The Gang That Couldn't Shoot Straight*; *The Godfather*," he said, turning them over. "They look good, Lieutenant Bradley. Thank you."

⁂

I was about ten minutes early at the café. It was at the edge of a busy market, and the traffic heading into Saigon was heavy. I thought I was going to be late, but Sergeant Borroughs had unexpectedly good knowledge of the area, and navigated the crowded streets with skill and dropped me off.

I ordered a coffee, and watched the masses of people as they bought fresh food, and met, laughing, arguing, and sharing whatever news they had. On the subject of news, I had picked up a copy of *The Saigon Post*, one of a surprising number of newspapers published, and read a long report of the previous day's bombings. There were three front page articles, all of them short on facts, and long on speculation. The countess was already nearly seated before I saw her.

"You are as pre-occupied with the news as I am," she said.

She didn't smile, and when she took off her dark glasses, she looked like she hadn't had much sleep. A waiter arrived, and she ordered coffee with some *croissants* and slices of *cramique*.

"I'm sorry I missed you yesterday," I said. "I didn't get to Saigon until after six."

She gave the sort of shrug that sulking teenaged girls gave in French films.

"This is the beginning of the end," she said.

"That's what the newspaper said," I replied.

"It won't be victory for the South, regardless of what the papers say," she said. "The Americans are already leaving, and when they're gone, no one will defend the terms of the peace agreement, if there is one."

"I think you're being very cynical," I said.

"I have lived here all my life. I remember the stories of Dien Bien Phu, and I remember what happened afterwards," she said. "We survived, or we didn't.

"The Americans have lost interest in this war," she continued. "It has cost them too much, in every way: in lives, in money, in prestige, and in political loss. That last one is the most important."

I considered this.

"Do you really think that after all those lives, and all that money, the US is really going to just leave Vietnam to its fate?"

"Yes."

I found it difficult to believe. The whole history of the involvement was to stop communism; the domino theory drove policy.

"You did your degree in history, didn't you?" she asked.

I didn't remember telling her, but I may have, otherwise Hawthorne must have, and if he did, what else did he tell her?

"Yes."

"Think about your own revolution; I'm a French citizen as well as Vietnamese. I've studied it, as we had some involvement," she laughed. "Yorktown was the last battle, but it wasn't decisive. Cornwallis surrendered, but he was not conceding defeat in the war.

"The war just. . . fizzled out because of a loss of interest and support in London," she continued. "That's what's happening here."

"And this offensive?" I challenged.

"The grand gesture that will enable the politicians to say they created the conditions for peace," she said. She looked at me carefully, then added, "Poor Bill; you Americans believe that anything's possible; in Europe and Asia, we have thousands of years that tell us it's not so."

Her voice had the slightly condescending tone, as one uses to speak to a slow child, but it was not unkind. I have since learned is the way Europeans tend to talk to Americans.

It was first time a foreigner had said, directly to me, that we misunderstood the world. I'd heard similar things from other Americans at college, and from anti-war protesters. Now, here I was, sitting in a café in Saigon, and getting it between the eyes at point-blank range. I had no argument to offer, so my only reply was to change the subject.

"Were you here the whole time, before and after Dien Bein Phu?" I asked.

"I did my *baccalauréat* in France, so I was away for three years," she said. "I lived with my mother's sister in Paris. I knew something of a normal life there, though most of my classmates thought I was odd."

"How did you feel about coming back to Saigon?"

"I was apprehensive, of course, but it is home."

The waiter arrived with coffee and a basket of *croissants* and the pieces of *cramique*. The countess immediately reached for a piece of *cramique*, tore off a piece, ate it, and smiled for the first time.

"Have one while they're still warm," she said, offering the basket.

"What did you do when you came back to Saigon?" I asked.

"I went to cookery school," she said. "There was a very good chef who had worked for the French colonial officials."

She smiled at the memory.

"He was well-known, and once the French were gone, catered for corporate events. Eventually, the major businesses persuaded the new government to use him for important functions, so he was back in the international circle, but he also began running the cookery school. It had French students like me, and many Vietnamese, too. Some are running restaurants now; others are still working their way up."

I was enjoying the hot morning, the coffee, *croissants*, and company.

"What do you do now?" I asked.

The countess looked at me with what I thought was distrust. It was the first time she had looked at me that way.

"You don't have to tell me," I said, casually, "but, we're

not spies."

She relaxed a little.

"I'm sorry. I'm not used to direct questions. Everyone here is circumspect, unless they're family," she said. "Let's just say that I work in an office, and sometimes with a catering company, with the chef I told you about. It's not exciting, nor particularly important. In the past few years, like you, my normal work has been interrupted by our exchanges, and carrying out the instructions you bring."

She looked down as she said this.

"Was there trouble?" I asked, after a moment.

She didn't reply. She looked around and waved for the waiter, and ordered more coffee.

"You don't know what these instructions are, do you?"

"I'm simply the messenger."

She nodded.

"Without going into detail, the last instructions were difficult," she said softly. "I'm not complaining, and it was within my agreement, but it was. . . difficult."

"I'm sorry."

As we finished our coffee, the sun moved to shine on us and the countess put on her dark glasses. I took the envelope and handed it to her. It was becoming the signal to terminate our meeting. I suspected it would take me time to get back to my ship, and didn't want to hang about Saigon longer than I had to.

I stood to leave, but she remained seated.

"Stay safe, Lieutenant Bradley," she said in an almost childlike way.

"You, too, Countess."

∞

"What did you make of that exchange?" Osgood asked.

"It gave me a lot to think about," I said. "First, her observation about the Americans leaving. Secondly, the biographical information that she shared, and finally, her comment about the last instructions being 'difficult.'

"It was the first time for thinking about several things, but primarily, it made me question what the papers I was giving her were telling her to do. Was I putting her in danger? It was pretty clear that the previous delivery wasn't radio scripts."

"And what were you thinking of the countess?"

Forty years ago, I couldn't have answered honestly.

"I stopped thinking of her as an operative, and more as a person."

"Was that because you had discovered she was Caucasian?" Osgood asked.

"No," I said. "It was because for the first time I saw her as being vulnerable."

Chapter VIII

Sergeant Borroughs had read about eighty pages of *The Godfather* when I went to his Jeep. Planes continued to circle overhead, and periodically, the noise would become suddenly louder.

"I should try to get back to my ship today," I said to him.

"I'll get you to the terminal as quickly as possible, Lieutenant," he said, starting the Jeep. "By the way, the book is very good."

He pulled into the traffic, and we barged ahead. There wasn't much he could do to accelerate the journey. He knew some shortcuts that saved us about five minutes, but generally, he just had to wait for the traffic to move.

As I suspected, there wasn't much COD traffic, but the ATO said he'd send someone to the Vietnamese Officers' Club to find me if the situation changed.

I went there, even though I wasn't hungry, and had little to do. I always left my journal locked up in my stateroom, but had a cheap spiral notebook, and drafted an account of the meeting.

The countess being vulnerable was a novel idea. She had previously radiated confidence, and even superiority at our previous meetings. I was teasing this out, and writing the draft when I became aware of someone approaching my table.

"Not still waiting for orders, I hope."

It was Colonel Myerson, the Air Force officer I had met on my first trip to Saigon.

I stood up.

"No, sir. I'm happily installed on the *USS Hartford* now. Can I get you a coffee, sir?"

He pulled up a chair and sat down, and I waved for a steward, and signalled for two coffees.

"When I left here, I went to the *USS Harrisburg*, but then, she went home, and I was transferred to the *Hartford*."

"Are you doing public affairs there?" the colonel asked.

"I'm helping."

"That's right, you were doing something spooky, weren't you? Is that why you're here?"

"One could draw that conclusion, Colonel," I said.

He smiled.

"And you, sir? Did you get your unit together?" I asked.

"Eventually. The boys are up there now," he said. "You

know what's going on, don't you?"

"I have pieced things together," I said. "Let's hope it works. How long will the campaign go on for?"

"I couldn't tell you even if I knew," he said. "I think it's going to be a long one, but I haven't been told. Are you headed back to your ship?"

"If I can get a COD."

"You might get something around 1700," he said.

"That would be a start," I said, looking at my watch and noting it was only 1230.

We finished our coffee and moved to neutral subjects.

"What about some lunch?" the colonel suggested. "I've got nothing on until I shake up the crews an hour before the squadron returns. The pilots were furious that all they were going to drop on Hanoi was chaff and propaganda. Hard to tell which is which."

He laughed, and, as he was a colonel, so did I.

Over lunch we talked of our home towns, college days and travel, but didn't hang around after we'd finished eating. I went to the terminal to see if there was any word on a flight and found that the colonel's "something around 1700" was an accurate prediction.

Having nothing to do, I went to the BX to see if it had any paperbacks worth picking up. I was surprised to see it decorated with Christmas lights, tinsel and signs, making it look like the big stores back home. Only the eighty-five-degree heat kept me from thinking I wasn't in Ohio.

I did find a few books, picked up some razor blades, and one or two other things that caught my eye.

I didn't mind waiting for transport, but I didn't want to have to spend the night on the *Midway*. As it was, I flew out at 1750 and landed on the *USS Enterprise* just after 2100, and was on a helo to the *Hartford* within fifteen minutes.

When I got to my stateroom just after 2200, I found Lieutenant Russo packing.

"Going on leave, Gordon?"

"Going home!" he exclaimed. "I'll be there for Christmas for the first time in three years."

"When do you leave?"

"Zero-eight-hundred tomorrow," he replied with a huge grin. "With any luck, with all the cuts that are going on, you'll have a private stateroom."

"I don't think anyone knows I'm here," I said.

"One day when you have nothing to do, find out who does the brass engraving on board and get a sign made that says, 'VIPs Only' and stick it on the door," he laughed.

Although I was exhausted, Gordon was excited and

wanted to talk as he squared away his belongings.

"There's a drawerful of stuff there. Have a look through and take whatever you want," he said.

By the time I woke up the next morning, Russo was long gone. I had breakfast, and checked in to public affairs and reviewed the recent photographs that had been done. I cross-referenced the pictures against the schedule, and selected a few dozen and marked the contact sheets for cropping.

After lunch, I went back to my stateroom and wrote up the meeting with the countess in my journal, and settled back to read my book.

CB

While I tried to make myself useful, I was well aware of the men who were risking their lives all over the country that was only one-hundred-twenty miles from my comfortable stateroom, and doing it every day, in terrible weather and conditions. All I can say in my defence is that I didn't have many days like this.

More to prove that I could get something done, I returned to PAO and asked if they knew who did the engraving on the ship. Of course, they knew. One of the journalists offered to handle the transaction for me, so I wrote down the size of the plate, and what I wanted engraved.

"What do you need to swap for this?" I asked.

The journalist smiled.

"A full colour picture of the ship usually does it, sir. We've got a drawer full of them."

I thanked him, and said I might have wandered the ship forever, looking.

"You know what they say, sir," he said before heading out. "Want to know something, call PAO."

"Call PAO," was something of a joke on the *Harrisburg*, too, so I shouldn't have been surprised it was also the case on the *Hartford*.

Calls could come at any time, but often, they'd come from the wardroom, the captain's cabin, or the admiral's mess, in the late evening. It would be after a big meal, and some good conversation that a question would arise, then a debate, then a bet. To decide this bet when no one present knew the answer, someone would say, "Call PAO."

When stateside, with telephone lines connected to the civilian network, it was not unusual to get calls from a bar. One question was always asked more than others:

"The *USS Arizona* still flies the American flag, but is it still under commission?"

We had a list of such questions stuck to the side of a filing cabinet, and that question had about seven hash marks next to it. We'd be asked about Academy Award winners; who was Franklin Roosevelt's third vice president; what was the last name of Alice in *Alice in Wonderland,* and other important questions. Occasionally, there would be questions about sports, and someone was usually able to turn up a book with the statistics and answer them.

Oh. While the *USS Arizona* does fly the American flag, it was struck from the register on 1 December 1942.

◌

The previous day might have been easy, but at 0615, Mr Griffith banged on my stateroom door just a little too hard, and told me to be in the XO's office in fifteen minutes.

He gave me my orders only saying that my helo would depart at 0645. My meeting was scheduled for noon at the railway station at Place Eugène Cuniac.

By the time my helo reached the *Enterprise,* its air strike had launched, and we could land immediately. With the deck clear, the COD was able to land shortly after my arrival, and I was on my way to Saigon within the hour.

Sergeant Borroughs met me, and drove me into the city. I had almost an hour in hand. I invited him to have coffee with me in a café on Boulevard Krantz-Duparré. I ordered us a basket of *croissants* and some *cramiques.* The sergeant had never had the latter before, and ate all but the one I had first grabbed.

He was a quiet young man who was making the most of his time in the Army, studying and learning new skills in his spare time. The subject that warmed him up the most was fishing. I knew nothing much about fishing, but since I knew Borroughs was a great reader, I asked if he'd read "Big Two-Hearted River."

His face lit up.

"No disrespect, sir, but I'm surprised you know that story," he said. "Say 'fishing', and everyone mentions *The Old Man and the Sea*, but "Big Two-Hearted River" is even better."

"There is more in it," I agreed.

"I re-read it once or twice a year, and I'd like to think I could take the time for that sort of trip when I get home from this war."

At about 1145, I walked to the station, leaving Borroughs to finish the last croissant. No location was mentioned, so I thought I'd have a look inside to see if there were any likely meeting places. Even in her traditional clothes, I was getting good at recognising the countess among the dozens of similarly dressed women. She was noticeably taller, and broader in the shoulders, but how obvious that was to anyone just casually looking, I don't know.

I walked back outside, and the countess was approaching the station.

"Good afternoon, Lieutenant Bradley," she said formally.

I was in the process of returning the greeting when she held out her hand for the documents.

"Are you all right?" I asked, trying to see through her dark lenses.

"I told you yesterday, I'm frightened. The bombings are still going on, and it's going to stir things up in ways the Americans haven't dreamed of."

The manner of her speech was opposite to its content. She sounded perfectly calm, and relaxed.

"Can I help?" I asked.

She smiled.

"Get back to your ship, and stay safe," she said, continuing to hold out her hand for the envelope.

I gave it to her, and she turned, walked across the square, and disappeared in the crowd.

Sergeant Borroughs was surprised to see me back so soon. He was discreet, but permitted himself the odd comment.

"I thought you'd have lunch."

"I was too full of coffee and *croissants*," I said.

I was back on the *Hartford* in time for dinner.

ၹ

"Did you think it odd that she disappeared so quickly?" Osgood wanted to know.

"I was a little disappointed because it was nice getting to know her, but this was serious enough business to warrant a lot of time and money to arrange my trips," I said.

"And what were you thinking of that business at the time?"

I had reviewed my journals before meeting Osgood, so the memory had been refreshed.

"The period of Linebacker II was intense. I was pretty sure that what the countess and I were doing was closely related to those events, but how, I never knew," I said.

"Never?"

"We'll come to that," I said, borrowing one of Osgood's tactics.

"Just so," he replied.

"I was concerned about the countess' safety," I said. "I felt that the instructions, or orders I was delivering were putting her in danger. She expressed unease from time to time, but never in specific terms.

"The other thing I wondered about was her social life: I had the impression that she was very lonely. I could see why she might feel that way: the survivor of the *ancien regime*, as it were, and with no apparent family, parents or siblings. Did she have a boyfriend? She never mentioned one, but we were professional contacts, not friends."

Osgood raised an eyebrow.

"That's the hard thing for new agents to get used to," he said. "If you think of your contacts as friends, it makes it very difficult to kill them when you need to."

The remark shocked me the first time I heard anyone make it, but after a career in intelligence, I was used to the idea now, and saw its necessity. Mercifully, I wasn't asked to kill the countess, nor she, me – which was the far more probable eventuality.

"Go back to the countess," Osgood said. "Did she ever say where she lived?"

"No, apart from saying where her parents had lived. She may have still lived there. I sometimes had curious ideas about her living in a semi-derelict house, a remnant of colonial days, with elegant proportions, and damaged details."

"It may have been true," Osgood said. "What about friends?"

"She never mentioned any. Occasionally, she'd mention

a colleague at work, but only in general terms: this one was fussy; that one was irritating by the way she wouldn't share stationery; another one would hum while typing; that sort of thing.

"Why do we try to construct lives from so little information?" I asked rhetorically. "You see someone, and you automatically try to place them in a job; a social position; a type of life."

Osgood actually chuckled.

"And you learned that to be a good operative, you had to discipline yourself only to see and hear what was there, and interpret that, and suppress the fantasies, romantic and otherwise," he said. "Some people can never do it; you were lucky that you acquired that skill – eventually."

Chapter IX

We were starting to get news reports of the bombings of Hanoi and strategic targets, and even a
number of the officers on the *Hartford* were surprised by
the scale and intensity. There were rumours that we'd be
firing on positions later in the day.

I was still considering the countess' cynical observation
that this push was to pressure the negotiators, but once
the deal was done, the Americans would leave the South
Vietnamese on their own.

We were only a few days from Christmas, and even those
who had been on Yankee Station before found it difficult
to reconcile the mid-summer weather with the idea of
Christmas. With the proximity of the holiday, and the
activity of the bombing, I didn't expect another trip to
Saigon until after Christmas, and after the bombing
stopped, but when I saw Mr Griffith outside the wardroom door, I knew I'd be travelling again.

At least I had time for lunch before the 1400 helo. I connected with the COD on the *USS Ranger*, and I was met
by Sergeant Borroughs around 1700. The *rendez-vous* was

for 1800 at the first café the countess had taken me to.

Borroughs was more talkative that day, and the journey passed quickly.

"After talking to you the last time, I found a copy of 'Big Two-Hearted River', and re-read it," he said.

I had done the same. Finding Hemingway stories in a ship's library is not as hard as one might think.

"What did you think this time?" I asked.

"It gets better," he said.

"You notice more," I agreed.

"Nick must have had a tough time in the war," Borroughs said. "All the memories are kept down; you can tell by the way he focuses on what he sees and hears. It's all in the present. He doesn't compare anything to something from the past; he can't face it."

"Ever try writing something of your own, Sergeant?"

"With stories like that around, I don't have to, sir."

He dropped me near the entrance to the *cul-de-sac* where the café was. The countess had just arrived and was choosing a table. She was wearing a bright, flowered *áo dài*, and looking very *á la mode*.

She smiled when she saw me, and took off her dark

glasses. I was pleased to see her happier than at our previous meeting.

"I hope you didn't have trouble getting here," she said.

It was hard to judge whether this was a genuine comment, or an ironic one.

"I have an excellent travel agent," I said. "Flights, drivers, hotels, you name it."

She smiled, but then her face grew more serious.

"It's getting harder to get food," she said. "The farmers are afraid to travel. Prices are going up."

I knew that the economy, rocky at best, had been suffering even more since the peace talks began. It was the sort of thing that the Americans never noticed, with the regular supply lines from home.

The waiter came, and she ordered.

"I've asked for some chrysanthemum tea," she said. "It's very refreshing."

She was quiet for a while, enjoying the evening sun.

"What would you be doing now, if you were at home?" she asked.

"Buying last-minute Christmas presents. Contacting friends, and arranging to meet them. Going to parties – and shovelling snow.

"You must find Christmas in the heat very strange," she said.

The chrysanthemum tea arrived. I hadn't tasted anything like it before, but it was refreshing, and I liked it.

"Are you spending the night at the base?" she asked.

This question was on the edge of being an operational one, and immediately put me on my guard.

"It depends what time we finish here," I said.

"There's a small cinema that shows French films sometimes," she said. "I don't get to go often, because I don't like to go alone. Would it interest you?"

"My French is very bad," I said.

"You might be lucky, and it will have subtitles," she said. "We can have something to eat afterwards."

There was no reason for me to turn this down. Her reasons were credible, and I would keep on my guard. I didn't think there would be much risk, so I agreed. She knew the time the film started, so we finished our drink, and left the café.

Sergeant Borroughs was waiting around the corner. I left the countess for a moment, and told him to book me a room at the BOQ, and meet me back here at 2200. He responded with a simple, "Yes, Mr Bradley," and started the Jeep.

The cinema was very small, holding only about a hundred people. It was a simple shop with a small vestibule. The screen was about fifteen feet wide, but there were real theatre seats. We were given a small sheet of paper with the actors and production credits, and a short paragraph about the film. There was no popcorn, or other refreshments.

"*Le Charme discret de la bourgeoisie*," I read. "Luis Buñuel."

I had heard of Buñuel, and seen *Un Chien Andalou* when I was in college. You can imagine how that went down in Ohio when it first came out, but it was the 1960s, and people were more willing to be indulgent.

We sat about two-thirds of the way back, because even with the slight rake, we were both taller than nearly everyone there. I had thought that the countess might see someone she knew, and I might find out her name, but she went unrecognised.

The film did have basic subtitles in English, but the English was very bad, and the subtitles were several seconds behind the action. It gave the movie an even more surreal effect.

When the lights came up, I was disoriented. An American watching a French film in Saigon, with a woman whose name I did not know.

The countess didn't speak until we were a block from the

cinema.

"Are you hungry?" she asked

I nodded.

"Good."

She led the way to the restaurant, which was fairly near the café, so I'd be able to find my way to the Jeep. It was a large restaurant with tables on the pavement, but we went inside. I couldn't tell whether it was strictly Vietnamese, but it was certainly oriental, and stylish. Almost wordlessly, the countess was shown to a table, and we were given large menus. There were white table cloths, and western cutlery as well as chopsticks.

The menu was in Vietnamese and French, so I folded it and asked the countess to order for me. A pot of hot tea was placed on the table along with traditional cups. The countess waited for about a minute before pouring.

"Do you like talking about movies?" I asked.

"Usually," she replied.

"Not always?"

"I like talking about films to people who know what they're talking about," she said.

I laughed, but took that as a warning.

"Are you going to start?" she prompted.

"I liked it," I said. "I won't pretend that I understood all that was going on, and I am sure there were things in the French dialogue and manners that a foreigner wouldn't get, but it was clever, and wonderful social satire."

"In what way?" she asked.

Merde. I suspected she was laying a trap. I was given a few moments to consider how to reply when the waiter came to take the order. The countess engaged in quite a bit of dialogue with the waiter, questioning him about the food; pointing to things on the menu, and nodding towards me.

When she had finished, she looked at me and raised an eyebrow that signalled that I should begin my answer.

"One thing was . . ." and I launched into a comment I believed, but was probably too obvious. She was kind enough to nod in a few places, then questioned me on a detail, or symbol. Some I had caught; others floated by without notice.

"You must remember that I was trying to read very bad subtitles that were out of sync," I objected.

Eventually, she ended my misery saying, "You must see it again when you can speak French."

I drank some tea in the hope that it would alleviate the sting.

"Are you very bored?" I asked.

"Now?"

"No, in general. Is your life fulfilling?" I asked.

It was her turn to retreat to the tea.

"May I answer that after dinner?" she asked softly.

She offered a few thoughts about the film and Buñuel, then moved on to talk about Goddard, Renoir, Rohmer, and Truffaut.

I mentioned that I had seen *Monsieur Hulot's Holiday*, and she laughed.

"You cannot imagine how close that is to holidays in France," she said. "I went to a place very like the one M Hulot goes to with my aunt. The dining room was like a funeral parlour - "

"Like the restaurant in the movie," I interrupted.

She laughed again.

"It could easily have been like that. There were couples who never spoke; single people who made no effort to speak; and people who burned themselves so badly in the sun on the first day that they were never seen again," she related. "Then on the beach, there were people wrapped in robes and towels, so the sun never got near them, along with those who seemed to swim back and forth all morning."

"Did you meet anyone nice?"

"One always meets at least one nice person on holiday," she said. "But like most times, you or they are usually leaving the next morning, so in spite of trading addresses and promising to write, one never does. When you live in Amiens, who wants a girlfriend in Saigon?"

"Countess, you're an attractive lady; surely you had other opportunities," I said.

She looked at me, I thought sadly.

"That's another subject for after dinner," she said.

Dinner arrived as she said this, and the dishes kept coming: some open, some covered; some placed on candle-heaters, others direct on the table.

"What have we got?" I asked, surveying the feast.

She talked me through the dishes, and made suggestions on what should be eaten with what, and how the variety of sauces should be used.

"*Bon appetite*," she said.

I made the chopsticks work for most things, but for the larger objects (some of which I really didn't want to know too much about) I resorted to a knife and fork. What had looked like a quantity for half a dozen people, disappeared embarrassingly easily. We took our time, and chatted more about the movie, our favourite films, and she told me more about Paris.

While she loved the city, and enjoyed studying there, she claimed not to have formed many close friendships. I was sceptical, but she said that even though it was only half a dozen years ago, she was in touch with no one.

"What did you do when you got back to Saigon?" I asked.

"It was the summer of 1964. I had my *diplome*, and what passed for a good education, but, in reality, I was fit for very little," she said with a laugh. "So, I got married."

○੨

Osgood interrupted me at this point.

"Before the romantic interlude, there's quite a lot there that needs examination," he said.

"What hasn't been talked about?" I asked. "And why now?"

Osgood looked at me with painful tolerance.

"We need to assess any danger should we allow the countess to come to Britain," he said. "People who were very junior functionaries then are now in very important positions. They cannot be compromised by youthful indiscretion or incompetence."

"Very well," I conceded. I was never going to deter Osgood, so I stopped obstructing him.

"Have you reported all she said about the bombings?" he asked.

"Yes. She said remarkably little apart from saying it was the beginning of the end," I said. "It surprised me at the time, but I think it was more a matter of being sick of it than anything else. What she said later about her husband made some sense of that."

"We'll get to that later," Osgood said. "And you said nothing about the bombing yourself?"

"No."

"Tell me more about Sergeant Borroughs," Osgood said.

"Not much more to relate. He was quiet but personable. More at home in the country than the city. He had good mechanical abilities, which I put down to being a farm boy," I said. "He liked reading, and, like many readers in the military, read just about everything he put his hands on. He seemed to know Saigon extremely well."

"Was he assigned to the motor pool?"

"I don't know. I assumed so."

"Was he always your driver?"

"I had a different one once," I said. "I don't remember much about him. He hardly spoke at all."

"Did it ever occur to you that Sergeant Borroughs was Army Intelligence?"

"No. Even if he were, he wouldn't have learned much from talking to me, or from watching the countess and me," I said, "and not much more if he could hear us."

Osgood shifted in his chair, and poured another brandy.

"Do you think you crossed the line, going to the cinema? Having dinner? Exchanging personal details?" he asked.

"No."

Osgood looked pained, and tried to keep it from affecting his voice.

"Please elaborate."

I poured more brandy for myself, took a sip, and when I thought he'd waited long enough, replied.

"As I said, we weren't spies, or at least didn't consider ourselves spies."

"*You* may not have been a spy," Osgood said with obvious irritation, "but you had no idea if the countess was."

"As you suggested, I presumed we were on the same side," I said. "Therefore, I assumed that whether I preferred *Le Genou de Claire* to *Ma Nuit chez Maud* made little difference to the outcome of the war. Nor did I think it important whether we held hands or not."

"*Did* you hold hands?" Osgood said, looking up from his drink.

"You may find that out in a future episode," I said.

Osgood gave another of his sighs.

"I know this is ancient history to you, but it's something I have been asked to look into again," he said.

"Perhaps I'd take it more seriously if I were being paid for my memoires and confessions."

"Bloody hell," he said, more in resignation than anger. "I'll see what I can do."

In Osgood-speak, "I'll see what I can do," was a pretty firm assurance.

"I can feel my memory improving already," I said.

"Good. Now, tell me about the movie house: did the countess know anyone there? Did she talk to anyone? Did you sit with anyone?"

"Funnily, I remember this very clearly because it was the first thing we did together besides drinking tea or coffee.

"She seemed to know no one there; we didn't sit with anyone, and apart from the ticket seller, she spoke only to me," I said.

"Very good. Please continue."

Chapter X

As you will imagine, the countess' revelation about her marriage greatly surprised me. There had been nothing to prepare me for it: she wore no wedding ring; she made no excuses to leave early or do anything because her husband was waiting, or was expecting her, or would worry.

I'm sure I looked surprised, but the countess appeared to be absorbed in her own thoughts.

"I had known my husband before going to Paris," she resumed. "My mother was good friends with his parents. Our grandparents knew each other, too."

"Were they French?" I asked.

She nodded.

"They were, but they had been in Vietnam for two generations. Claude's father was a very highly placed official before the French defeat. He was well liked, and very able, so, like my father, he was employed by the new government, but at a much lower position and salary," she explained. "They all believed that the French had fortunes hidden away and didn't need to be paid much. It was also a way of humiliating them."

"Did they?"

"Humiliate them?"

"Have fortunes hidden away?"

She gave me a long look.

"To some people, it may have looked like a fortune," she said.

"And Claude?"

"Poor Claude," she said sadly. "He was just an official. He did liaison work with the Americans.

"He was a kind man, a few years older than me; honest, able, and wasted in Saigon," she said affectionately. "He should have gone to the École Nationale d'Administration in Paris and been a real high-flyer."

She paused, and I wondered if she'd say anything more.

"Do you want to know the whole story?" she asked, knowing the answer. "The Americans know it, so I suppose it's all right, but let's get out of here."

She waved to the waiter for the bill, and passed it to me.

We walked a few hundred feet down Boulevarde Krantz-Duparré to a café.

"You're close to my age, so you will want to know the things I'd want to know," she said, "not the boring things the American did."

"Do you know the name of the man who recruited you?"

She looked at me for a moment, wondering how I could interrupt her romantic story.

"Melville," she said, then continued. "I had a small, but lovely wedding. Everyone was happy. Claude was handsome, proud, and very, very happy. This was in January 1965. I was still eighteen. *I* was happy. I looked beautiful, and was the centre of attention.

"Was I in love?" she asked rhetorically. "Enough to marry Claude. As I said, what else was I going to do, living in a lost colony? I didn't see anywhere else I'd be any happier, and I thought we could have a good life, and maybe move to Paris."

"*Is* your life happy?" I asked.

She was wearing her inscrutable face, but even so, I saw the shadow fall over it.

"As I said, Claude was a government official, liaising with the Americans. That was what he was doing on 30 March 1965," she said.

"He was at the American embassy," I said, knowing what she'd say next.

"He was one of the two dozen killed," she whispered.

The bombing of the embassy was sensational news. It had

galvanised opinion in the United States, and provoked the acceleration of the deployment of troops, raising the number from around 35,000 to 184,000 between the bombing and the end of the year. That acceleration continued at nearly the same rate until the middle of 1968 when there were half a million US soldiers in the country.

"I'm very sorry," I said.

"We all were."

"How did you cope?" I asked.

She shook her head slowly.

"I didn't."

She looked at her coffee, and was very still for a long time.

"It was a bad time. I was a widow in my teens; I had nowhere to go; I couldn't stay where Claude and I were living. My mother was dead. She had hung on until she saw me married," she said. "I didn't know how ill she was."

"So, you were already mourning for your mother when your husband was killed," I said.

She nodded.

"I felt my life was over, as the cliché goes; but, believe me, it felt that way. I wore nothing but black," the countess said. "Melville made me stop when he recruited me."

She gave a little laugh.

"The traditional Vietnamese dress for bereaved families is white, but being French, I wore black."

"*La mariée était en noir*," I murmured. "I'm sorry; that's insensitive."

She smiled.

"It's how I thought of myself," she replied. "When I started this work, I decided to become less conspicuous. By adopting Vietnamese dress, I could still be in mourning, but in white."

"When did he recruit you?" I asked.

I didn't know if she'd answer, but the question seemed not to bother her.

"About six months after Claude was killed," she said. "I needed to do something. If nothing else, it would relieve the loneliness."

"Weren't you working?"

"Nothing anyone could seriously call work," she said. "I was working with the chef on catering jobs. I had stopped doing that when my mother died in February, and had only done a few jobs before taking another two months off to try to put myself back together."

With both my parents still alive, not yet having married, these were experiences I couldn't imagine.

"How did Melville find you?" I asked.

She shook her head.

"I always thought it was an embassy connection," she said.

"Has something caused you to change your mind?"

"No. I still think it was that," she replied.

She seemed convinced, but I was learning that the countess was a larger unknown quantity than, in my innocence, I had supposed.

"Are you working with more than one contact?" I asked.

Again, it was a question I thought she'd refuse to answer but she replied without hesitation.

"No. I've worked with a number of contacts; all from the Navy, but only one at a time." She hesitated before adding: "That gives me quite enough to do."

We'd finished our coffee, and I sensed we'd come to the end of our meeting. I opened my portfolio, and handed her the envelope. She took it with an expression of resignation, and put it in her large fibre bag.

I continued looking in my portfolio at a small oblong box, and debated what to do. I took it out and handed it to her.

"I don't know if I'll see you again before Christmas," I said, and gave it to her. "I don't know what you'll be doing, but I hope you can be happy."

Her face was expressionless, but she took it, put it in her bag, and stood up.

"Thank you, Bill," she said so softly that I could hardly hear her. "*Joyeux Noël*."

∞

Osgood took a deep breath. He had poured himself more brandy while I spoke.

"There was a great deal of what you Americans would call 'unauthorised' conversation at that meeting," Osgood said.

"Not really, old boy," I said, teasing him with the ancient epithet. "Hawthorne asked me to act as a courier. I knew I wasn't supposed to open the envelope I was supposed to deliver, but nothing was said about topics of conversation, or flirting with my contact."

He pursed his lips, but made no comment. I sensed it was a struggle.

"Nothing was said about dinner or going to the cinema, either," I added.

"All right!" he exclaimed. "It's not as though you haven't told me this before, but let's pick it apart."

I helped myself to brandy.

"Were you surprised to find the countess was married?"

"It never occurred to me that there was an earl or a

count," I said.

"Do try to be serious."

I could tell I was irritating him. Since he just agreed that he'd try to get me on the payroll again, I controlled my impatience. Though, after turning sixty, I found myself doing things I'd never have dared to do in youth.

"As I related, she showed no signs of being married. No ring, no indication that she needed to get away; no unconscious references," I said. "On the other hand, we hadn't met that many times."

"So, it didn't occur to you that you were going to the cinema, or to dinner, with a married woman?"

"No. Nor with a widow," I added. "You will have seen all this in her file; in Hawthorne's notes."

Osgood made no comment.

"What would have made him think she'd be a good operative?" I asked.

"You tell me."

"All right," I said, thinking. "Young. Physically healthy, and presumably fit. French, so apt to have fixed loyalties. Intelligent. Vulnerable after the death of her mother and husband. Possibly in need of money."

"Would that have persuaded you?"

"No," I said. "I don't think mere money would have persuaded me."

"What did persuade you?" Osgood asked.

"It was put to me as an order."

"But the countess didn't have to follow orders," Osgood suggested.

"There was some leverage? That makes sense. What would have worked?" I considered, speaking mostly to myself.

I thought a moment.

"Promise of rescue in the event the South was lost?" I suggested, but was not wholly convinced. "If she had the fortune, she would have been able to leave on her own, if not to Paris, then at least to somewhere safer, like Manila, or a nearby French, or former French, colony."

"Not bad, Bradley. You haven't let your brain rot," Osgood said with a rare smile. "Now, let's move on; we can take that one further later."

"The next thing you'll want to know is, did I think there was a fortune?" I said. "Who knows? She was always well dressed. Hair, nails, make-up all carefully done; probably professionally. This was her *persona*: the countess. Elegant, but not obvious, careful attention to detail; impressive, but an image to convince, not to impress."

"Very good!" Osgood exclaimed.

"I thought the *persona* was her armour; a protective shell. But, you know, I wondered for the first time that night if it was a disguise. Was she like this in her daily life, or did she only dress up like this for our meetings? Was she afraid friends and acquaintances would recognise her if they saw her with me, or the Americans before me? I thought that dyeing her hair was something she did normally. I'd heard of European women doing it in Asia, especially blondes. They got sick of people touching it for good luck. She told me her hair was a different colour, but didn't tell me what."

Osgood laughed.

"So, what do you think was under the countess' mask?" he asked.

"Vulnerability; like most people. She's alone, in a city about to collapse, an outsider," I said. "She let the mask slip later, but we'll come to that."

"All right," Osgood said. "How emotionally strong do you think she was?"

The question surprised me, as at that time, I had no reason to consider it.

"Apart from the normal bruising that close deaths cause, I think she was slightly stronger than average. Of course,

I don't know what the instructions I gave her were asking her to do, but I saw no ill effects," I said. "She was always in perfect control during the course of our meetings. The news, and sometimes the odd thing I said disturbed her, but that's normal. She hadn't been recruited – or trained – to be a sapper."

"That's true," Osgood said. "What about the fortune hidden away? Did you ever learn more about that?"

I laughed.

"We Americans are more forthright than you English, but even we seldom go that far. She had described it as 'a fortune to some,' and never mentioned it again," I said. "I don't think that she was hard up, but I didn't know how much the ministry was paying her."

"Money was going into an account at the Hong Kong & Shanghai Bank, in Saigon," Osgood said.

"I wish I'd been paid that way. Mine was going into an account in London," I complained, not for the first time. "It was years before I saw a penny of it."

Osgood sighed, and moved to his next topic.

"Did the countess ever give any indication of the questions Melville asked her?"

"The 'boring things'? No. I assumed they were the sorts of things he asked me; though he had met me informally on the ship, and probably gathered more information than I realised at the time."

"You never met Melville," Osgood said, surprised.

"I'm not as dumb as I look, even back then. I might have read history, but I knew that Herman Melville was one of Nathanial Hawthorn's best friends. There's no way that the 'American' who recruited the countess was named Melville," I said. "It may have been Hawthorne in disguise. He may have been a great one for Am Dram in the Home Counties."

"I thought it a nice touch," Osgood said. Then, his tone shifted. "Who did you think Hawthorne was?"

"On the *Surrey*? At first, I thought he was a business man who might have personally known the captain, or other senior officer. As the evening progressed, and he said nothing about business, and a good deal about regional current affairs, I thought he might be a visiting Foreign Office official.

"There was nothing directly related to events, the military, or operational matters, but a lot of talk around it," I continued. "It gradually came to me that he was more likely to be someone to do with defence than the Foreign Office."

"Did you say anything to him about that?"

"Not until later."

"How did he react?" Osgood asked.

"That was Hawthorne: he didn't react visibly to anything."

Osgood drew his chair back to the table, and put his elbows on it and stared at me.

"What did you suppose the countess meant when she said she 'had quite enough to do'?"

I know I had just said it, but I tried to remember the actual scene from decades earlier.

"I think I considered it a flippant remark; the sort young people make. They may not be wholly true, but they help convey an impression of one sort or another."

"Quite so," he said, without expression. "And what sort of impression did you think she was trying to make?"

"Now *that* I do remember," I said. "I thought she was suggesting that with her job, and taking time to meet me whenever ordered, find food during the current shortages, and keep up appearances, that her life was full – even though, as I said, I suspected it was not."

"A reasonable assumption. Did you ever know for certain that she had a job?"

"No."

"She never asked you to meet her at her place of work?"

141

I shook my head.

"No."

"Did she ever give an indication of where in the city her office was?"

"Again, no."

"Did you never suspect that meeting you and carrying out the instructions was all she did?" Osgood pressed.

"No. I thought she simply delivered the contents to the relevant people," I said. "It hadn't occurred to me then that these were actually orders for her and that she was more than a courier."

"Indeed," he said. "Tell me, you gave her a Christmas present. What was it? And, what prompted you to get her something?"

"I had a pretty firm feeling that she was lonely. To some extent, so was I. I didn't yet have any close friends on the *Hartford*, where I was still considered an outsider.

"I'd gone to the BX at Tan Son Nhut that time I'd been delayed, and everything was decorated for Christmas. I'd shipped a box to my parents a few weeks earlier, and had nothing else to buy, and no one to buy it for, but there was some nice jewellery, and very inexpensive. I picked out a gold chain with triple circular links. It came with three disks that could be hung on to it. They allegedly displayed the Vietnamese symbols for blessings, prosperity and longevity, but they could have said, 'I hate Madam Nhu.'"

"Why did you buy her a present?" Osgood asked.

"It was the season. I wanted to do something for someone; she was the obvious candidate, and I liked her."

"Were you falling in love with her?"

"No," I said.

That was later.

Chapter XI

Christmas on a Navy vessel while underway is painfully like any other day. There was a late start (0900) so that anyone wishing to attend religious services could, and there was an extended allowance for lunch (half an hour extra). Otherwise, the routine of work continued.

The food on the mess deck and in the wardroom was special, with steak and lobster-tails for all. There was a Christmas tree in the wardroom, and the men in the PAO/Admin space had strung some lights and streamers, and had Christmas cards from home on the file cabinets, or on the bulkhead by their desks. For some, it was their first Christmas away from home, and they were feeling strange and homesick.

In admin, the men organised a "Secret Santa" and these presents were exchanged after lunch, and half a dozen of the junior officers I worked with did the same. I was the recipient of three paperbacks, which were gratefully received.

After lunch when I returned to my desk, there was a small

present on it, with a tag that only said, "Merry Christmas." I opened it with a little caution, as I was aware I was being watched. It was the brass plaque I'd asked for, with "VIP Suite Private" engraved on two lines. I turned to the three men who were there.

"This is perfect! Thank you!"

"We've got some double-sided tape, so you can put it up," one of them said.

"Much appreciated."

Christmas music was playing on the eight-track player for the rest of the afternoon, and apart from wondering how the countess was spending her day, I continued the work on the cruise book.

For those unfamiliar with them, a ship's "cruise book" is like the yearbook of a large high school. Pictures of everyone are included, along with good photographs of work on the ship, the ports visited, major events, distinguished visitors and VIPs. These are strung together with a loose narrative that provides an *aide memoire* of the chronology of the deployment. Nearly everyone orders a copy; the ship's welfare and recreation fund pays about half the costs, while the crew pays five or ten dollars. It's a lot of money to be accounted for, and on carriers, the costs can be tens of thousands; there are stories of cruise book money disappearing when someone involved is separated from the ship.

On Christmas night, the ship's closed-circuit television ran one of its newer movies, and the men in office sat together chatting, watching the film and eating popcorn.

ↁ

Mr Griffith took pleasure in waking me at 0600 the next morning with instructions to see the XO at 0615 and be prepared to leave the ship at 0630. I knew there had been no helo landings since 2000 Christmas night, so the XO, or Lieutenant Griffith, had been sitting on my orders since then. It was pointless to say anything, but I filed it away for possible future use.

I was at Tan Son Nhut by 1000 having made a quick connection on the *Saratoga*. The faithful Sergeant Borroughs met me and drove me to a café on the river. It was about a mile up from the hotel, and in an area I didn't know.

The heat was exceptional for the time of year and was expected to hit ninety-five degrees before the day was over. Borroughs showed me where he'd be waiting, and drove me to the café, around the corner.

It wasn't a particularly picturesque scene, but it may have been a hundred years earlier. There was considerable river traffic of all sorts. Small wooden boats, coasters, and military vessels navigated closely together, and occasional angry blasts from horns could be heard above the sound of the traffic.

The sunlight was hitting the café, and even under the green awnings, it was breathless. I'd only been there a few minutes when the countess arrived. She perfectly mimicked the unwesternised native walk; it was hard to describe, and it may have been pretty much the same across the Orient, but it wasn't the languid, or determined striding of western women her age.

"*Bonjour*," I said as she sat down.

She gave a slight smile, and looked for the waiter. The dark glasses remained in place.

We ordered coffee, but the countess declined the offer of anything to eat with it.

"The bombing raids appear to have stopped, but the stories from the countryside are terrible," she said.

"Is there food?" I asked.

"A lot of places were shut yesterday, but there is more talk of shortages than ever," she replied. "That doesn't mean there are real shortages, but in this environment, that hardly matters; the fear makes it real."

The coffee arrived, and we drank quietly as the combination of heavy trucks and planes low overhead made conversation impossible.

"Tell me about Christmas on the ship," she said, when it

was quiet enough to resume speaking.

I related what it had been like; how strange for many of the sailors, but how most had made the best of it.

"I'm glad," she said. "Mine was almost like any other day. I was afraid to go to midnight Mass, but then thought, what did it matter if I was killed. So, I went. It was lovely, but I knew virtually no one there. Shopkeepers, people from offices I knew, a lawyer, a few old teachers, but no friends. They've gone.

"I made lunch for an old French lady who lives across the hall from me. We listened to some old records of French café songs and looked at back issues of *Paris Match*. She still gets it, somehow. The newest ones she had were from October."

She didn't often say things in a sarcastic way, and it amused me.

"The best thing was a friend gave me a pretty necklace."

She opened the high collar on her *áo dài* and showed me.

"Thank you. It was a kind thought."

"I hope it doesn't turn your neck green," I said.

She surprised me by starting to giggle. Apart from an exclamation of amusement, she seldom laughed, and I'd never seen her actually giggle. She took her dark glasses off to wipe her eyes, and she looked younger than ever. I don't know if it was just the laughter, or if she had changed her make-up, but the mask was gone, and she looked like a young French girl enjoying a morning in a café.

It didn't last long, but it showed me what she could be, if given the chance to flourish. When her face grew serious again, I was startled by what she asked me.

"Do you know anything about what's going to happen?"

It was almost a plea.

"I don't know anything," I said.

"Will the heavy bombing start again? Is anyone saying how long it will be before the Americans are gone?"

I shook my head.

"I'm sorry, Countess," I said. "I'm not in a position to know anything."

"Well, what do you do when you're not driving the boat?" she demanded.

I started to tell her, but then said, "Not much."

She looked disappointed. Disappointed in me; and it hurt.

"I told you, I'm just a messenger," I said. "You might be more, but that's all I am.

"I've thought a lot about what you said," I continued.

"About the Americans leaving. It goes against everything I believe about America, but I'm afraid you could be right: a peace agreement will be signed; the Americans will go, and who knows what provisions will be made for your country's defence."

She held out her hand for the documents. I took the envelope from my document wallet and passed it across.

"This is getting harder to do," she said, but didn't give me a chance to reply. "Promise me something, Lieutenant Bradley: that you will never lie to me."

"I promise."

"Don't say it too easily. The time might come when you will go home and will leave me behind. Promise me you'll tell me when you're leaving."

"If I know, I will," I said.

She stood up, and I followed.

"Countess," I said, and she turned back to me. "You're not Madame Butterfly."

Her face was totally blank for a moment.

"No, I'm Princess Turandot."

ଔ

"Well that all sounded perfectly straight forward," Osgood said with as much irony as I'd ever heard him use.

I was about to answer when a waiter approached the table.

"Forgive me, Sir Julian," he said. "The Bennett Room is free. This room must be prepared for the dinner service."

Osgood looked up. It was one of those curious reversals where the man who was about to rebuke me was being told to leave the room by a waiter.

"Right you are, Hazlett," he said with good humour. "Come, Bradley. Bring the bottle."

I stood and reached for it, but Hazlett stopped me.

"That won't be necessary, sir."

He followed us to the Bennett Room, which was little more than an antechamber, had a table with some chairs. It was lit by a chandelier in perfect scale to its relatively small size. Hazlett placed the bottle and glasses on the table, and silently closed the door as he left.

"Where were we?" Osgood asked.

"You were about to berate me for my frivolity forty-five years ago," I said.

"Well, you must admit that it was somewhat indiscreet."

"What part of it?" I asked.

"Promising to tell her if you were leaving. That could have been an operational secret."

"It could have been, had I told her," I said. "If you remember, I didn't."

"No. What did you feel about that meeting?" Osgood asked.

"I felt that the countess was becoming distressed about being left behind," I said. "For all her outward serenity, she was apprehensive. It was as though she was realising how alone she was. If the Americans left, and Saigon fell – as I think she realised would happen at that stage – she'd be without anything to do, and little or no income. After all, she'd been doing this work – whatever it was – for eight years. No doubt, she was afraid of that being discovered, too."

"What did you think was going to happen?"

"To her, or to Saigon?"

"To Saigon," Osgood said.

"America had never left a war unresolved before," I said after considering it. "I had no reason to expect it to do so now. If a peace accord could be reached – and Operation Linebacker II showed the level of commitment to getting one – then it was unthinkable that a military provision would not be made to enforce it."

I thought Osgood was beginning to look tired. As if on cue, the steward knocked on the door and entered with a tea service and some cakes. He silently put it on the table and left.

"I like this club," Osgood observed almost jovially. "No superfluous word is spoken."

He ignored my answer until we had our tea, and were into the first piece of cake.

"I think we all suffered from that delusion," he said. "Letting Saigon fall undid a lot of the work that you and the countess did."

I didn't question this. If he planned to tell me, he would. Asking wouldn't get any more information out of him.

"How did the countess' apprehension manifest itself?"

"In the first two months I'd worked with her, she was friendly, but professional. With the start of the bombing, she became more personal," I said. "At first I put it down to the fact that we were getting to know each other better; that some trust was developing; and we shared the fate that we were young people caught up in a war we didn't want to be part of.

"After the start of the bombing, it was as if she sensed this was the endgame. Perhaps she related it to stories from her family of the days leading up to Dien Bien Phu. She now had no family, few friends, and didn't want to see the life she'd been leading disappear completely.

"For all that, I never heard her make any political comment," I added, as it came to me. "Nothing about decisions, incompetence, corruption – anything. She didn't criticise the Vietnamese, the Americans, the French, or the British."

Osgood poured more tea as he pondered this.

"Do you think she was trying not to burn bridges?"

"Possibly. I don't think she believed that I was as unimportant as I was."

"It's good you never lost sight of that," Osgood said, not completely frivolously. "Would you have kept your promise?"

"My 'indiscreet promise'? Yes. If I knew I was leaving, I would have said good-bye. It's only proper."

Osgood grimaced.

"There's a time and place for good manners," he said.

"And there was nothing to make this improper," I countered.

He gave me a look of tolerance. Possibly his worst condemnation.

"There was no reason not to tell her I was leaving," I argued. "She had worked with other contacts before. There could have been one after me."

"Come! Even you knew that was unlikely. So, did she."

"But it's not a reason not to tell her. Was she owed not even that? Perhaps not by you, but she was by me."

Osgood waved a hand.

"Very well. Your point."

"Her concern and questions did make me think more about my own future on Yankee Station," I continued without acknowledging his comment. "The *Hartford* had been on Yankee Station for several months before I came aboard. It wouldn't be long before it received orders to return stateside. The bombing campaign had ended, so it was a logical time to rotate or retire ships. I didn't think it was imminent, but then again, I didn't think the fall of Saigon was imminent, either."

"Knowing the big picture would not have reassured you," Osgood said. He shifted in his chair, and changed his tone: "What did you mean to imply by saying she was not Madame Butterfly?"

"That she was not a helpless woman who would be left behind, and forgotten," I replied easily.

"And what did you make of her response?"

"That she was an ice-queen."

Osgood nodded.

"Have another cup," he said, pouring.

Chapter XII

A t the beginning of the month, I was commuting to Saigon twice a week. Then it was three times a week. With the cessation of the heavy bombing, the only carriers left on Yankee Station were the *Ranger* and the *Midway*, so connections were not as frequent, but I seldom had to wait two hours.

The frequency of the meetings, and the less efficient connections meant that the time with the countess was usually short. We met, had lunch or a drink, and I handed over the envelope.

Commercial passenger jets and military transport planes were taking soldiers back home. On the few trips that I needed to stay overnight at the BOQ, it was virtually empty, as was the Vietnamese Officers' Club, unless it was over-run with departing personnel.

Several members of the admin and PAO staff received notices of large cuts, up to six months, and I knew it wouldn't be long before the *Hartford* received its orders to return home.

As well as being shorter, the meetings with the countess

had become frosty, reflecting her self-identification with Princess Turandot. That mythical princess had grown to disdain men, and was seen as unapproachable. Her hand could only be won by the man who could answer three riddles. One of the riddles was, "What is like ice, yet burns?" The answer is Turandot; filled with anger, cold, and ruthless. Suitors failing to answer correctly are beheaded. I wasn't expecting that fate, but just about anything else was possible.

We continued to meet at various cafés and restaurants. I no longer knew how she would behave when we met. Sometimes she wanted to chat; other times, it was a quick coffee, and she'd hold out her hand for the envelope.

She kept her mask, and no longer gave anything personal away. This withdrawal of engagement, of course, made her more attractive. She made me feel that I'd betrayed her in some way, but I knew I hadn't. What she was trying to achieve by this, I didn't know; it may have been simply a self-preservation strategy, but I missed our more relaxed conversations, and meals.

It's sheer vanity to think that she'd felt anything for me, and probably delusional that I felt anything real for her. All we really had in common was loneliness and fear, and the confrontation of an unknown future; the typical ingredients of wartime romances, but she seemed determined not to let that happen. The one hope I had that she still felt something was that she continued to wear the choker I'd given her.

One day in the third week of January, when I met her, she told me to drink my coffee quickly. I did, and she started to walk down the street. We were in a neighbourhood that I had not been to before. It seemed to be away from the central spots and familiar landmarks; those places that would have been tourist magnets in peacetime.

"You've not really seen Saigon," she said. "You should see some of it while it's still here."

She led me through a tangle of narrow streets that smelled of fresh food, cooking, and industrial processes. It was alive with people shopping, standing in clusters talking, doing business, or drinking in small bars, bakeries, and cafés. Street food was available everywhere, and the countess pointed out several curious Oriental delicacies.

This was not a rich neighbourhood, yet the people were clean, and well, if frugally, dressed, and industrious. We walked for about a mile in a large circuit in which I saw shops of every kind, and tiny mechanical operations: grinding, machining, printing, metal working, casting, shoe and dress-making, and weaving of cloth, palm leaves and bamboo. As we walked, the countess led me by the hand for short distances before dropping it, it was a practical way of not losing me, not an expression of affection.

We walked unnoticed and without hindrance. Occasionally, the countess would stop and speak to someone working, presumably asking what they were doing, or talk about business.

We tasted small portions of grilled meat, fish and sweetmeats, vegetables wrapped in leaves and pastry, and fruits I'd never seen before with flavours I don't have the language to describe. Finally, in a tiny café that was mostly on the street, I was introduced to egg coffee, one of the most delicious drinks I've ever had.

As we emerged from the narrow streets and alleys onto the wide boulevard that took us back to the café, the countess spoke.

"This is what will be lost when Saigon falls."

Her certitude that the city was doomed continued to surprise me.

"All the ordinary people earning small amounts of money, but doing work of their choosing, and making it their own," she continued. "I think people reach a stage in their lives when they look back to see what they have accomplished. If there is something to see, or to at least know, then I think people can see a good life.

"The man who served us the fruit: he probably serves five hundred people every day. Some love his fruit, some will leave it after tasting one or two pieces. But if he works six days a week, that's more than one-hundred-fifty-thousand people he's fed in a year. He can be proud of that," she said. "My grandfather was a bureaucrat for forty-seven years, and he could point to nothing that he had accomplished. I think that's sad."

She was clearly moved by these thoughts.

"I think you're wrong," I said. "He could point to your mother and you, and say he provided for you; fed; educated, and kept you all safe, and prepared you for the world. He played a big part in making you, and watching you grow must have given him pleasure."

I could tell she was staring hard at me even though I couldn't see her eyes. Her face was impassive, cold.

"I'm glad he doesn't know me now," she said, and walked on.

We returned to the café and had a chrysanthemum tea. Although she sat with her customary, Oriental stillness, I could tell she was agitated. It was a studied stillness, not one of calm. I was learning to read her, although the signals were very subtle.

She was genuinely Oriental in her manner, though she may have been Western in thought and attitude. I was also learning that she didn't like people to get too close. It wasn't a question of being a woman of mystery, but of one who didn't want to be discovered.

"Do you like opera?" she asked, suddenly.

I looked at her with some surprise.

"You mentioned *Madame Butterfly*, and didn't question my *Turandot* reply," she said.

"Everyone knows *Madame Butterfly*," I said. "I had to look up *Turandot* when I got back to the ship."

"Have you heard it?"

"No," I admitted.

"It was one of my grandfather's favourites," she said. "That, and *Samson et Delilah*. He had old records of them that only played for a few minutes. I think he liked that one because it was French."

"Do you like opera?" I asked.

"My aunt took me a few times in Paris. She wanted me to like it, so introduced me gradually. *The Marriage of Figaro*, then *Don Giovanni* – they're easy to follow and fun to watch. Then, she took me to *Ariadne auf Naxos*; it was a bit of a risk, but the first part is funny, and the melodies are wonderful."

"Why are we talking about opera?" I asked.

She didn't take offence at the question, and, I think, saw the near absurdity of it in the circumstances.

"I was thinking of the lives with little to show, and I remembered Donizetti. He wrote almost seventy operas, but died in a mad house. Every night, he'd dress up in his formal clothes and wait to be called to the orchestra pit. Against the triumphs he'd known, I think that is heartbreaking."

I had been to the theatre enough to be able to imagine the excitement, anticipation, and anxiety of an opening night. Donizetti had known many such occasions, while the works performed remained, the countess noted that there was nothing of the event; the experience; *le melieu, ou le moment.* (Something else I had to look up.)

This was unfamiliar territory for an Ohio boy, more used to hearing about corn and hog prices, so I just asked questions that I hoped were intelligent. It was far removed from the traffic and noise overhead, but that may have been the point.

As the month continued, the weather became more variable, which affected both my helicopter and COD flights, as well as the venues for our meetings. We had two meetings inside steaming, noisy cafés before the countess suggested we meet at the Majestic (Hoàn-Mỹ) Hotel.

The countess was looking increasingly tired, and I still

had no idea of the content of the envelopes I was giving her.

The stream of Americans continued to leave on every available aircraft. Pan Am and TWA 707s and 747s, C-130 transports fitted with airline seats in addition to the webbing. The number of soldiers visible in Saigon was noticeably lower, and a quiet tension, blended with a sense of resignation surfaced from time to time. The countess expressed a prescient sense of abandonment, which I tried to assuage.

"What are you going to do? Smuggle me aboard your ship?" she asked impatiently one afternoon.

I thought of the three empty bunks in my stateroom and the "Private" notice on my door, and wished I could.

"Just give me the envelope, Bill," she said.

∞

"What was the talk aboard the *Hartford*?" Osgood asked.

"There was a sense of excitement," I said. "The feeling was that Linebacker II had worked, and those remaining in the office were expecting news of cuts in their service on a daily basis. Many were hoping that a peace accord would be in place in time to have an impact on their time left on active duty.

"This was not unwarranted, as Ensign Gumerie had been

notified of his imminent departure a week earlier," I said. "He was very disappointed. He had about two-and-a-half years to go, and had hoped to be a career officer. He took the idea of being chucked out while still an ensign very badly. The men thought he was crazy to try to get the orders changed, but no dice.

"The churn continued with new officers and men coming on board regularly to make up the billets."

"You used the term 'endgame' earlier," Osgood began. "Did you sense it then?"

"Yes and no," I said. "The cuts fostered that feeling, but I had no expectation of an early departure or return to civilian life."

"And how did the countess' attitude affect you?"

"It made me feel helpless."

"You wanted to rescue her?" he said.

"Yes," I said. "But not for myself. Just to give her a better life; a chance to live in peace."

"In America?" Osgood challenged.

"France would be the more likely place. Somewhere she'd feel more at home," I said. "America never occurred to me. With French and, possibly, British citizenship, those were the obvious places for her."

"You never imagined her in Centerburg?"

"Not seriously," I said. "Paris was her best bet, I thought."

"Your comments reflected a romantic disposition," Osgood said. "What were your feelings towards her?"

"Ambivalent. I was always too pragmatic about my girl-friends. Anyone who lived too far away, didn't stand a chance. Still, having regular contact with an attractive girl was rare while on active duty overseas, but it was just a business relationship," I said. "I admit that the more time I spent with her, the better I liked her, but I didn't really know her, or what she was doing."

"Was she behaving differently during this time?" he asked.

"I think her fear that she'd be abandoned caused her to become more distant, more formal. Maybe she even resented me for that," I said.

"You said she took your hand."

"Only to lead me, or make sure I didn't get lost."

"Were you getting more questions about your activities?" Osgood asked.

"The XO no longer spoke to me, but handed me the envelopes with a curt good morning. The PAO and Admin crowd accepted my disappearances as normal. And when I wasn't visible, no one looked for me," I said. "I had the feeling that if the orders stopped coming, I could stay in my stateroom until the ship was decommissioned, and no one would realise I was missing."

"And then, things changed," Osgood said, leading me to the next phase of my story.

"And nothing has been the same since."

Chapter XIII

What happened next startled everyone. On 28 January, the announcement came that the peace accord had been signed in Paris, and that a ceasefire had begun. All American troops would be out of South Vietnam in sixty days.

My first instinct was to talk to the countess, but no orders had come for me. I knew that she would think that this would hasten the fall of Saigon, and increase her peril. I could only hope that she had some way of contacting Hawthorne, or someone in MI7 on my behalf.

I had little doubt that this agreement would also throw a spanner in whatever the British were doing. It had taken me a long time to work it out, but I thought my suspicions were sound.

In the office, the news had come through late on January 27. One of our friends in Comms leaked it to us, and we soon received it on the teletype service that the ship's Electrician's Mates hacked into on behalf of PAO.

For the next two days, I received no orders. It was hugely frustrating, especially because I was anticipating that the

Hartford would receive orders home any day. To distract myself, work on the cruise book continued, and I had sent off several sections to the publisher.

Ensign Gumerie moped about trying to rethink his career plans. I was less than useless to talk to, having no idea myself what might come next. In my case, I suspected there was still a fairly good chance of not getting home alive.

On February 1, I went to the wardroom for an early breakfast. Lieutenant Griffith found me there just as I was finishing my pancakes and sausages. He looked unhappy that he was unable to interrupt my meal.

"The XO wants to see you ASAP," he said.

It was all he ever said to me.

The XO didn't say much either, but handed me the latest envelope which I took back to my quarters before opening. I was to go immediately to meet the countess at the Majestic Hotel at 1100.

In addition to those normal orders, there was a separate envelope for me.

> *Dear Lieutenant j.g. Bradley,*
>
> *You are instructed to prepare to leave the USS Hartford at a date within the next seven days. Reservations will be made for you at the Majestic Hotel. Your*

stay there will be brief, and you are advised to travel lightly. One small bag is your allowance.

Please arrange for any other possessions to be shipped to your home from the USS Hartford.

You will receive subsequent instructions at the Majestic.

Destroy this message.

There was a signature "pp Hawthorne."

The redoubtable Borroughs met my flight, which arrived leaving only the minimum amount of time to get to the hotel on time. I had taken half a dozen paperbacks with me to give to Borroughs. It would save sending them home, and he would enjoy them.

"Have you received your orders home yet, Sergeant?"

"Not yet, sir, but I'm looking forward to them," he answered cheerfully.

"Planning a fishing trip?"

"I tied some flies over the weekend, sir," he said.

We were quiet as we drove into town. The humidity was high, and I wanted a shower after just sitting in the car. The countess, however, looked as cool as ever.

"Have you been waiting long?" I asked as I sat down.

"Only a minute or two," she said.

Being inside, she was not wearing her dark glasses. There was no disguising that she was worried, and probably had not been sleeping.

"How was the news received here?" I asked.

She looked down, sadly.

"Everyone knows it's over. The only question is how long can Saigon hold out."

"How long?" I asked.

"Opinions vary," she said, bitterly. "Once the Americans are gone, six weeks to three years is the range."

I sensed that this would be soon translated into being my fault.

"How are you keeping?" I asked.

She looked around the room, at the ceiling and out the windows, as if to say, "What a bloody stupid question!", yet she answered calmly.

"I have been sorting my things, and putting those things I need and want to keep into a suitcase, but whether I get the chance to use it, I have no idea."

"I'm packing, too," I said.

I couldn't see that this was a risk, but I wasn't going to tell her everything.

"We're expecting the ship to be ordered home any time,"

I said. "I don't know if I'll be ordered to go with it, or to do something else, so I've begun sorting things, too. I just gave Borroughs a pile of my old books."

"If you don't go back with the ship, how do you get things home?" she asked.

"We can ship things at very favourable rates. Some are boxed. and airlifted off and flown back. Other things will stay on the ship until it reaches an American port and be sent from there," I explained.

"So many things to consider," she said.

"I don't have much," I said. "Some books and tapes. Civilian clothes. Not much else. I haven't been anywhere to acquire things."

She smiled.

"You ought to have some sort of souvenir of Saigon."

"I'm open to suggestions," I said.

She didn't reply, but drank her coffee. When she put down her cup, she stood up and held her hand out for her instructions.

"I'm sorry we don't have more time," she said, enigmatically, and left.

Sergeant Borroughs met me at the door and drove me back to Tan Son Nhut, and I returned to the ship.

With only time for a wash, I went to the wardroom for dinner. I hadn't eaten since breakfast and was starving. When I saw Lieutenant Griffith, I knew it would be a while before I ate again.

"The XO wants to see me," I said, before he could open his mouth.

"It's not a good idea to be a smart-ass," he said.

"I'm sorry, sir. What was it you wanted to tell me?"

"The XO wants to see you," he said, and glared.

"Thank you, Lieutenant."

"Sit down, Mr Bradley," the XO said when I entered his office.

I thought he looked more relaxed, though the ship continued to maintain its state of maximum readiness.

"I am pleased to learn from Mr Gumerie that you have made yourself useful," he began. "I don't like having people on board that I don't have control of, and neither does the captain."

"I understand that, sir."

"Apart from using our helicopter as your private vehicle, you have been minimal trouble."

"Thank you, Commander."

"The *Hartford* received some good news this afternoon.

We're going home."

I started to react, but he held up his hand.

"This will be announced at 2000, and I expect you to treat this as Top-Secret information until then," he said. "I have orders for you, and have been advised of your next movements. You will separate from *Hartford* at 1200 tomorrow. That will give you time to pack, and package your things. You will continue on TAD to the British Ministry of Defence until further notice.

"That is all."

He handed me the envelope, which felt thicker than usual, but whether that was my part, or the countess' I didn't know.

I returned to my stateroom and opened my orders. They repeated what I had already been told, but filled in dates and times. I was to report to the Majestic Hotel where further orders would be delivered, as Hawthorne's note had said. I was to take with me only what I could comfortably carry.

I was not happy knowing that while everyone else was going home, I would be remaining behind – and for what?

With no indication where I was going, I realised I had to take most of my uniforms, which left little room for anything else, and no matter how carefully I packed, every-thing would need ironing before wearing.

The men in PAO were a tremendous help is organising boxes and shipping instructions for my other stuff. They made it their priority business the next morning, and everything was sealed up, labelled and delivered to the ship's post office by 1000.

I distributed more books, tapes, and stationery equip-ment to the PAO and Admin teams, including half a dozen carbon typewriter ribbons I'd locked in the back of a drawer.

I gave my stateroom key to Mr Gumerie.

"Why don't you move in for the duration. If PAO retains the key, it can be at your disposal. TJ will keep it clean and change the sheets, and it's unlikely anyone will think to put anyone else in there," I said. "I'm sure you can get one of your pirates to arrange to have the lock changed."

I gave him my Ohio address and told him to let me know what he decided to do. I paid my wardroom bill, and handed in Ensign Gumerie's key, giving his stateroom number.

At 1200, I lifted off from the *USS Hartford* for the last time, not realising that it was the end of my duty with the United States Naval Reserve.

∞

Osgood was starting to look weary. It wasn't his age, but the knowledge that the easy bit was over, and that he was about to confront the more controversial aspects of the countess' story – and mine.

He fortified himself by adding more hot water to the tea pot. "What was your reaction to the news of the peace agreement?" he asked.

"I was delighted, but could not believe that the war I'd heard of throughout my teenaged years and beyond was over," I said. "I also thought of the countess' comments about leaving the country to its fate."

"Did you feel that way?"

"Not really," I confessed. "I could see her point, but it had been a war that was recognised as being unwinnable for a long time. I didn't see another realistic option."

"What else were you thinking?"

"I was feeling in no-man's land. I was going to live in a hotel, for I didn't know how long; I'd be separated from the shipboard routine and colleagues, and I'd be away from the military command that had been protecting me," I said. "It gave me an appreciation of the countess' position."

"What did you think would happen?" he asked.

"Not what did."

Chapter XIV

Sergeant Borroughs met my flight and drove me to the Majestic Hotel. I gave him a few last books and magazines; my others had gone to the PAO crew and the ship's library.

A room had been reserved for me, and the clerk handed me a large envelope along with my key. My room was on the fourth floor with a good view of the river, and a small balcony. I opened the doors to let fresh air in, even though it was hot and humid. It would be raining within a few hours.

After hanging up my uniforms, and putting my remaining few books on the bedside table, I opened the envelope. It was taped shut and sealed. A second similar envelope was within, and I opened that one, too.

This contained my orders to leave the *Hartford*, and told me to remain at the hotel until I received further orders. It also said I would now be paid the per diem rate, which everyone in the military covets.

The third envelope contained the standard meeting message. This one told me to meet the countess at the hotel at 1730. I looked at my watch. It was already 1725. I changed my shirt and smartened up in time to walk off the elevator and into the lobby at precisely 1730. I remembered David Niven's entrance into the Reform Club, "Well, gentlemen, here I am."

The effect was somewhat spoiled by the fact that the countess wasn't in the lobby, but in the bar. She was at a quiet table in the corner, but had not yet been served. She looked unhappy, sitting on her own, and reminded me of the girl in the impressionist painting, alone in the café.

"Lieutenant Bradley," she said as I approached. Her eyes did not brighten when they saw me; I had become the bringer of bad news; the reminder of destruction.

"Countess," I said, returning her coolness with warmth and a smile.

I resisted the temptation to kiss her hand, but might weaken as our meetings drew to an end. Whatever *my* fate, I did not think I would be left in Saigon.

She conceded a small smile.

"And what do you think of the news now?" she asked.

"I think our lives are going to change," I said cheerfully.

"That's what I am afraid of," she said.

"You like your life now so much?"

She gave me a look of tolerant exasperation.

"I am free," she said. "My life isn't great, but it's mine."

The waiter came, and we ordered.

"I'm living here now," I said.

She looked up.

"My ship is going back to the US. I've been left behind to work with you."

She didn't seem to understand.

"Work with me?"

"Well, no more than before, but they want me to stay, and continue to do what I do with you," I explained.

The countess considered this. The phrase "work with you" seemed to disturb her, making me wonder, once again, exactly what she did. With the winding down of the AFRTS broadcasts, I was now certain that it was more than delivering radio scripts.

"Did you manage to pack all your things?" she asked.

"The guys in the office were great; they helped pack stuff and get the paperwork sorted out," I said. "I just have one bag with me."

"You have instructions for me?" she asked.

"Just the normal radio scripts," I said, passing over the envelope.

She nodded as if to say, "Okay, if that's how you want to

play it." She took the envelope and put it in her bag.

"I don't like being here," she said. "People assume that Vietnamese girls in hotel bars with Western men are prostitutes. I can do without that image just now. When the communists come, they will take the leaders, the professors they think are liberal, the writers, and the prostitutes."

"I've been in worse company," I said.

She glared at me, stood up and left. I didn't try to stop her, as it would have made a scene. Besides, in a few days, she'd be ordered to see me again, and we'd go somewhere else.

There wasn't long to wait. At breakfast in the hotel dining room, I was handed an envelope by Sergeant Borroughs who had driven in with it. I invited him to have a coffee with me, but he declined and departed.

At 1100, I waited outside the hotel for the countess. She was wearing a flowered *áo dài* that I hadn't seen before.

"We can go to the café around the corner, or somewhere else," I said.

She smiled.

"No, we can go inside. I was in a bad mood yesterday," she said, and took my hand and led me in.

This nice one day, foul the next was typical high school

behaviour. Either the countess was bored, or something else was going on. I knew I wouldn't get it from her now, and would just have to wait for her to tell me.

"I haven't seen that dress before," I said. "Is it new?"

She shook her head.

"No. It's actually fairly old," she said. "Like most women, I have a number of clothes that I keep for special occasions. I didn't like the idea of leaving them when they'd only been worn once or twice."

I didn't ask if she was that certain she'd be leaving them behind, then realised that it was a better option than having them taken from her.

We ordered cold drinks, and waited until we were served before talking.

"It's getting close, isn't it?" she asked.

I looked uncertainly at her.

"The end; it's close," she said. "You know that; all your ships, and planes, and men – they're all going. And you? Do you know the timetable? When Saigon will be no more?"

I couldn't answer her; I had no answers for myself, let alone her. She always refused to believe me when I protested my ignorance.

"I don't know when I am leaving, countess," I said as convincingly as I could. "For all I know, I'm expendable."

"Like me?" she demanded.

There was no reply to that one either.

We sat quietly drinking for a few minutes. I was surprised that she hadn't held out her hand for the envelope.

"Let's walk along the river," I said.

The countess looked doubtful, but stood without comment and walked out with me. It was hot, but not steamy, and there was the odd cooler waft of air from the river.

"When you were growing up, what were your dreams?" I asked.

I could see her stiffen, but she said nothing, and I waited. I'd had a Quaker as an English teacher in high school. Her ability to stimulate discussion by asking a question and saying nothing for minutes on end until someone broke the silence awed us. It was virtually one hundred per cent effective.

The countess and I walked several hundred yards before she spoke. She surprised me because she had a big smile.

"It was to go to Paris, of course," she said. "I told you about reading the old copies of *Paris Match*; well, that was going to be my life. I would either be a fashion designer or a chef."

"You came close with your cookery," I said.

She looked wistful, but shook her head.

"Paris was a wonderful place to be, but I learned that life, wherever you are, has the same daily challenges," she said. "I told you that I didn't fit in, but I only told you that I seemed odd to them. I didn't say how odd they seemed to me."

"How so?"

She didn't answer right away, and I feared she'd ask for the envelope.

"You may not have been able to notice, but this is an Oriental country."

I must have made a face, for she laughed.

"No, I am sure you've noticed the obvious things, but maybe not the way people think, and that's the most important difference," she said. "The first difference is the sense of time. It affects everything; the individual ceases to be important in the Western sense; lives are important, but, individuals are just part of the continuum of time.

"You're the historian, but I have the sense that in the Oriental mind – including mine, to some extent – it's similar to the Middle Ages in Europe."

I was intrigued.

"In what way?"

"It's as though lives are running on two tracks," she said. "One is the normal rhythm: the seasons, holidays, birthdays, the growth of children, and the dying of the old. At the same time, there is the sense of a greater pattern. It's what made the Mediaeval builders build the way they did. Buildings and institutions to last a thousand years – and so many look like succeeding: cathedrals, schools, universities, hospitals.

"Here, it's not buildings that last, but traditions, methods, ideas. What the West sees as irrevocable change with the advent of communism in China is hardly a few seconds in Chinese history. Here, the hatred of the Chinese is ancient, but strong. The communists may overrun the country, but not forever. The culture will survive, it may go underground for a century, but somehow, the essence will endure.

"Seeing people acting like there was no tomorrow, as you Americans say, was a shock," she continued. "It is superficially very attractive, but after a while I could see that it wasn't an attitude that could survive. I needed more.

"Many people may think that spending hours learning to make pastry is a waste of time, but pastry has been around for a long time, and people still recognise good pastry and bad pastry."

She laughed at her own seriousness.

"I do believe it," she said. "Things evolve, but they don't change. Life, love and death are the same as ever, and so are other things."

While I hadn't focused on the Middle Ages, I knew that the concept of time was much different than today. It was on parallel tracks, too: expecting the Second Coming at any moment, while at the same time, building for millennia. It showed a highly complex view of the universe with sophisticated ideas. I had read enough to know that the wonderful anachronisms found in Mediaeval and late Mediaeval art and literature were underpinned by the notion that all things exist simultaneously in the mind of God. Einstein must have had something to say about that one.

We reached a place where it was possible to sit on a low wall and watch the river traffic. The riverside was commercial and industrial with ships of all sizes, and tiny wooden and woven bamboo vessels. I watched with fascination as these small craft were expertly paddled with a single long oar, avoiding swamping by much larger powered ships.

"The woven bamboo basket boats and larger sampans have regional distinctions," the countess said. "One from North Vietnam would instantly be noticed here."

"Could you really sail one from the North?" I asked.

"Yes, it's probably done regularly," she said. "It's easier if there's a sail, but sails aren't as common as they were."

She talked about crossing the river with friends as a child, and how even at very young ages, children would go out in basket boats that looked like coracles.

"The long banana shaped versions are more common for fishing and transport, but there are still many round ones," she added.

She continued with various recollections, and never returned to the discussion of her dreams. I didn't press her, but stood with the intention of walking back to the hotel.

As I looked around generally, I noticed a US Army car parked a few hundred feet up the road from us. I had no doubt that we'd been followed, but whether it was Borroughs or someone else in the car, I couldn't tell. I didn't mention it to the countess, for she would not have found it reassuring, as I did, though I was surprised at the precaution.

She was quiet on the way back to the hotel, and took my hand. I remembered what she had said about looking like a prostitute, so wasn't surprised when she dropped it after a dozen or so paces.

When we reached the hotel entrance, she held out her hand, and I gave her the envelope.

"Keep safe," I said to her.

She gave the slightest of smiles, nodded, and walked down the road.

Chapter XV

I ate alone in the hotel dining room. The food was good, and included a range of local, French and pseudo-American dishes. I had a Vietnamese chicken curry, which used a lot of lemongrass, which I liked, but had not encountered before.

Afterwards, I looked around the bar to see if anyone interesting was there, then returned to my room to write up the day's curious conversations. The countess had managed to say a lot, but gave very little new away.

As night set in, my room felt very big and empty after my small stateroom, which even though I had it to myself, was cramped. Lieutenant Russo had noted that although it could not be compared to a sardine can, it could be likened to a corned beef can. The noise from the street was also in marked contrast to the near silence, apart from the hum of the ventilation system.

It was a slow transition back into the real world, and I had no assurance how long that would last.

When I finished writing, I took a book and went down to the bar and had a whisky. People came and went the whole time, but there were probably not more than a dozen at any one time.

Not knowing what the next day would bring, I resolved to go to bed at midnight. At least I wouldn't find Lieutenant Griffith lurking at my threshold.

ભ

The next morning, I went to the dining room for breakfast at seven. I had decided to see something of Saigon. I didn't have a camera, but wanted to at least explore the central area more than I had. I'd had fleeting glimpses of the courts, the Independence Palace, and the opera house. I well remembered the bombing of the Presidential Palace in 1962, the coup, and the subsequent visit of Mme Nhu to the United States. She was feted, but was judged to have made more trouble than she was worth, but it had been a propaganda victory for her. The new palace was a modern fortress with none of the grace of its 19th century predecessor.

As I walked around, I felt perfectly safe. No one paid any attention to me, and I enjoyed a late-morning coffee at a small shop that served pastries and sandwiches. There were hundreds of people going about their business with a cheerful efficiency, yet stopping for a few seconds to acknowledge friends, before hurrying on.

My dominant feeling was that I was doing nothing, and it

was an uncomfortable experience.

I had brought my book and read, and watched the crowd. Something the café owner was cooking smelled delicious, and people were starting to order lunch. I joined the line, and saw a row of fish grilling. It was coated and stuffed with something that made it look appetising. I ordered one. It came with some rice and sliced cucumber.

I have no idea what sort of fish it was; it could have been bass. Borroughs would be able to tell me. The coating was a mix of garlic, chili and the inevitable lemongrass. It had been rubbed into cuts in the side of the fish, and stuffed inside. I was given chopsticks to eat with, and it flaked off the bone easily.

While the meal was delicious, the ambiance had gone downhill with the arrival of dozens of people crowding to order. My table and chair were jostled, but a hasty apology almost always followed. The empty chairs were occupied, and spirited conversations I could not understand were going on inches from me. It was clear that this was now a place for eating and leaving, and not lounging, and taking up space. I didn't hurry, but left when I had finished and sought out a more European café for a *digestif*.

On my return to the Majestic, the receptionist handed me my key and an envelope. This was the small, cream coloured one that I was used to seeing from Hawthorne. It had nearly familiar writing on it, and was written in wet green ink. I came to appreciate that one's eccentricities were an important part not just of one's character, but of one's identity. In a world where it has, since then, become increasingly difficult to prove one's identity, such things were important markers. They also had the advantage of not being recognisable by machines.

I returned to my room, which in spite of the French windows being left open, was stuffy. I propped the door to the hallway open to see if I could provoke a breeze.

Dear Lieutenant Bradley,

You will have gathered that our work is in its final phase.

Please be ready with all your possessions at the river side of the hotel tomorrow morning at 0600. Do not bother checking out.

Sincerely,

Hawthorne

Like a death that is expected, the recognition of the finality was still a shock. As I packed my uniforms and few other possessions, I realised with profound regret that I had no way of contacting the countess. Would Hawthorne/Melville have contacted her, too? Or would she be left behind, as she feared?

The countess knew I was powerless, but nonetheless, I had made my stupid promise, and that I couldn't fulfil it would be a lifetime regret.

By dinner time, I had lost my appetite. I wrote more in my journal, arranged to be called at five-thirty, and went to bed. I knew my sleep would be fitful, and that by four I'd be awake, having dreamt of missing the pick-up, flight, train or other connection.

I left the hotel a minute before six and turned down the road that ran along the river bank. Borroughs was there in an open Jeep.

"Sorry, sir, there was no staff car available this morning," he said.

I put my bag in the back, and climbed in next to him. He drove off towards the air base in the still light traffic.

I glanced at him as we parted from the route I knew to Tan Son Nhut.

"Railway station, sir," he said.

I nodded. I'd been there, and it seemed that I'd depart from there. In the dim morning light, the city had a dreamlike quality about it: shapes rather than distinct buildings; the impression of a Hollywood set, with side roads that went nowhere, houses that were unoccupied, and empty offices with only the odd light on to mislead those who looked on.

We drew up in front of the station. I wondered if I should get out, but Borroughs gave me no instructions. We sat there for two or three minutes. Then, walking out the main entrance with a large, old leather suitcase, came the countess.

She wore her customary outfit: the white *áo dài* and palm-leaf hat. She carried a small embroidered handbag that looked more suited for the opera than an escape.

Borroughs got out of the Jeep, gave her a courtesy salute, and took her suitcase and put it next to my bag. He held her hand as she clambered into the backseat.

"Good morning, Countess," I said.

She gave a weak smile. She looked frightened, and as though she'd had about as much sleep as I did. I turned in my seat to face her, as Borroughs drove off. I should have got in the back with her.

"Do you know where we're going?" she asked.

I shook my head.

"Do you think we're going to the same place?"

Seeing her had been a surprise, so I hadn't got as far as thinking if we'd be going to the same destination. I could think of lots of reasons why we wouldn't be.

I reached back and squeezed her hand, and she held it for

a moment, until the Jeep bounced over a number of pot-holes and broke us apart. I turned to face the front, and recognised the route to the air base.

I didn't need to tell the countess where we were headed, but I couldn't tell her what would happen once we got there.

I had been spoiled by staff cars, and this Jeep ride was rough. The countess seemed unbothered, and sat with stoic calm as we rattled on. When we entered the air base, the smooth quiet of the road was a welcome relief.

Borroughs drove to the terminal building.

"I'll wait here with the cases," he said. "You can get your orders inside, sir; Ma'am. Then, I'll drive you to your plane."

"He's helped me since I arrived here," I said.

"He's the big reader?" she asked.

"That's him."

We went in and were passed from desk to desk, until we were shown into an office in a back area. There were a few metal chairs, a clear desk, a file cabinet and a tele-phone. There was a map of Southeast Asia on the wall with a variety of coloured pins stuck in it.

The countess sat quietly and said nothing.

When the door opened, I stood up and faced the Air

Force officer who entered.

"Good morning, Mr Bradley," he said.

"Colonel Myerson," I said with surprise. It seemed that the first person I met in Vietnam would be the last.

"Countess," he said, extending his hand to her.

She gave it a polite shake.

"We're all set for you," he said. "Your plane will leave in about half an hour. Do you have papers, Countess?"

She opened her clutch, and withdrew a folded cream sheet of paper and handed it to him. He read it, nodded, wrote something in the corner, and handed it back to her. She folded it and put it in her bag without looking at it.

"May I see your ID or passport," he asked me. "Just for form."

He checked both and returned them. The colonel then opened a drawer and withdrew two envelopes and handed one to each of us.

"These are your orders, passes, and other documents. You will be issued new ones at each stage of your journey. I can't tell you where your ultimate destination is, but I have been instructed to tell you that you will be travelling together until you are safely back in Western Europe."

I glanced at the countess, who I thought looked relieved. I felt certain that the colonel's instruction had come from

Hawthorne.

The colonel addressed the countess.

"For now, you will be in the care of the United States Air Force, 56th Special Operations Wing, which will fly you safely to Bangkok. Happy landings."

With this caricature performance, the colonel left us, and we headed back to the awaiting Borroughs.

There were several planes in the process of loading and boarding not far from the terminal building. Fork-lift trucks were taking crates into the back of a C-130, and a TWA 707 was being prepped for a waiting crowd of noisy GIs.

We drove along a road lined with buildings near vast aprons where a variety of planes was parked.

"That's yours," he said, pointing at a C-123 that had one engine running.

When we were near the plane, he drove up next to a building with USAF painted on its corrugated steel wall, and Borroughs parked on the side of the building away from the runway, about a hundred yards from the perimeter fence.

He stepped out of the Jeep and walked around to my side to get the suitcases. I climbed out and was looking at the plane, wondering where we'd be going, when I heard a crack and a short grunt.

I whirled around, thinking, "Not now!" and saw Borroughs' lifeless body lying half in the back seat.

Behind him was the countess holding a pistol.

I gaped at her hand with the gun, not understanding.

"It was my mother's," she said.

Chapter XVI

My incomprehension was total. I stared at the countess, and waited for her to shoot me, but she calmly put the pistol back into her handbag, and snapped it shut. She continued to wear her dark glasses, and her face was infuriatingly impassive. Finally, she nodded at Borroughs, and seeing his body objectively for the first time, I saw the .45 1911A1 pistol in his hand.

"Come on!" she said urgently, taking her suitcase.

She walked purposefully towards the plane which was showing signs of imminent departure. I followed quickly. An Airman took our cases and secured them at the rear of the aircraft, and soon we were belted into webbed seats along the fuselage. The doors were closed almost as soon as we had settled.

There were about two dozen soldiers and the odd civilian on board. The civilians had the tech-rep look about them, and had been talking until the second engine started, and conversation became impossible. Down the centre of the aircraft an assortment of wooden crates had been secured to the deck.

I was aware of furtive looks at the countess and me. I turned to her.

"Take your dark glasses off," I shouted in her ear.

She looked at me quizzically, but took them off. Those who had been looking, now looked with more interest, and less suspicion, even though she still had a .25 Beretta in her handbag.

It was impossible to talk, and I didn't know whether to be grateful or frightened. Had Borroughs really been ready to kill one or both of us? In which case, the countess had saved my life. Or, had he seen her gun and drawn to defend himself and me?

The plane taxied sluggishly to the end of the runway, then the engines went from a roar to a whine. When we started to roll forward and accelerate, the countess held my arm and leaned her head against my shoulders, and apart from some minor movements as the plane encountered turbulence, she remained in this position for the duration of our flight.

When we landed, she put on her dark glasses again. Our cases were put on the tarmac, and we collected them and headed to the military terminal. The Don Muang Royal Thai Air Force Base was a shared facility with commercial airlines using the same runways. The United States military also had an area, and there was considerable security to prevent unauthorised access in either direction between civilian and military sectors.

We were directed to a US Air Force building, and then to an unmarked office. I was certain that Borroughs' body had been discovered and reported, and expected we'd be on the next flight back to Saigon, and charged with murder.

A Major Murdock greeted us.

"Welcome to Bangkok," he said.

Unasked, we handed over our papers. He read, signed, and dated the countess' letter, and checked my passport and military ID. After returning them, he opened the office door, and called to a clerk who worked at a desk in the open office.

"Sergeant," he called, and was followed back into the room by a young Airman.

"I am sure the countess would like to freshen up after her trip, can you look after her. She may want some things from her suitcase," the major said.

The countess rose silently, and followed the Airman.

"We're not used to many women, but there are some facilities for nurses," he said. "It also gives us a chance to complete the formalities here."

There was nothing sinister in his manner, and he seemed

to know how things should be done.

"There is one problem," he said, and I waited for the blow. "You will be flying out on a commercial flight, but it's been delayed until 1500. I expect you are both hungry. Did you manage to get anything to eat before you left Saigon?"

I shook my head.

"I don't expect the countess did, either," Murdock said. "Airman Pacelli will take you to the officers' mess, and you can wait in the lounge area there until your flight. It's pretty basic, but I think you'll be comfortable enough.

"Since you are flying commercial, the countess will need normal civilian papers. She may also want to change out of her Vietnamese costume, but that's up to her," he said.

"Here is a French passport, or near enough, in the name of Françoise Mauriac. She's a journalist for *La Dépêche* in Toulouse. Anything else, you or she can make up," he said. "This envelope is for you. I have your orders, and a letter from the newspaper explaining that Mlle Mauriac is a freelance writer commissioned by the newspaper. That is why she does not have a press pass on this trip. They are harder to arrange than passports.

"Good luck, Lieutenant," he said, standing up.

I thanked the major, and went outside to wait for the

countess and Airman Pacelli.

I just hoped she hadn't shot him.

☙

I opened the envelope and read my orders. We would fly from Bangkok to Calcutta on a TWA flight. We'd have comparatively comfortable seats, a meal, some drinks, and perhaps even a film. After the C-123 flight, it sounded luxurious.

I put the papers away when I saw the countess approaching. Airman Pacelli was still alive.

"I'll take you to the officers' mess, sir," Pacelli said, as the countess put some things back into her suitcase.

It was a short walk, and after the Jeep ride, and the basic seating on the plane, I was glad to stretch my legs, though the smell of avgas, and roar of engines spoiled the fantasy of a country walk. The countess, behind her dark glasses, felt more distant from me than ever. I was sure she was still scared, and I had no way of knowing how she felt, having just murdered a US serviceman. As I walked, I realised that my silence on the matter had made me complicit, and possibly an accessory after the fact; aiding her escape; harbouring a fugitive, and so on. The TV shows replayed themselves.

Airman Pacelli left us at the door to the officers' mess,

and we went in. Lunch service was buffet style, with stewards serving drinks, clearing plates and fetching special orders. There was a complete assortment of table arrangements ranging from long tables of a dozen, round tables for six, and square tables for four. There were enough empty tables for four that we signed in with the supply officer in charge, served ourselves, and took our plates to a table about as private as possible.

When she sat down the countess took off her dark glasses. She looked strained, but otherwise, her colour was good, and she ventured a slight smile.

I ignored the obvious topic, deferring it until after lunch. Borroughs was dead, so discussion of it could wait a few more minutes.

"I don't know where we're ultimately going," I said, but we're flying out at three o'clock on a TWA flight to Calcutta. My orders don't go further than that," I said. "I think it would be a good bet that we're going to Europe, as Colonel Myerson said."

She nodded.

Neither of us was enthusiastic about eating, but once we'd started, the level of our hunger showed itself.

"I've also been given a French passport for you," I said. "This will make your travel easier. I suspect the picture is one Melville took."

"What's my name?"

"There is a good cursory cover for you. You are Françoise Mauriac."

"Pffft. A Gascon," she said.

"You are a freelance writer on a special assignment from *La Dépêche*. Major Murdock said you could make up any supporting details, but to keep them minimal," I said.

"Not a bad cover," she said. "I suppose you think you're in a spy story now. May I see?"

I handed her the passport. She flipped through it.

"It's very convincing," she said. "It shows my flight from Toulouse to Paris, and my arrival in Saigon. The dates are conveniently blurred."

I hadn't looked at it, but was impressed. Being a government agency that didn't exist obviously had its advantages. I held out my hand, and she returned the passport.

"What's your cover story?" she asked. "Why are we travelling together?"

I hadn't thought of this.

"I leave it to you to make something up."

She gave a smile more like herself, and finished her meal. She didn't want dessert, so I left her to check the lounge area to see if there was coffee there. There wasn't.

A steward asked if I wanted something, then told me he'd bring coffee in when we'd finished.

One end of the room had a large worn rug and a few armchairs that looked like they might have been donated by departing personnel. From there we could have a good view of the room, and our conversation would be difficult to overhear.

When we were settled with our coffee, I turned to the countess.

"Please don't hate me," she said.

"Just tell me what happened, Countess," I said.

"I am much more suspicious than you," she said. "I've had to be. I've lived with danger, but usually it doesn't involve me. While choosing what to bring with me, I found the old pistol. My father gave it to my mother and taught us both how to use it. I was about thirteen. There are ranges where you can learn and practice for not much money.

"I can strip and clean it, but not terribly quickly," she said. "Anyway, when I found it in the back of a drawer, I asked myself if my father would want me to take it with me, and I decided he would, so I slipped it in my bag."

She looked around.

"You know, I'd love a cigarette."

I asked a steward who produced a service pack of ten, and

paid him.

"I smoked in Paris, of course," she said. "Everyone does. I don't smoke much, but once in a while, it helps me relax."

She went through the ritual, and eventually had one lit, and inhaled.

"For some reason, you weren't speaking to Borroughs. I'd never met him, but understood that you and he had running conversations about books, movies, fishing and such things," she said. "So why not this morning? I thought you'd sensed that something was wrong, and that put me on my guard. I watched him, and for a someone who had driven you so often on that route, he seemed very tense. His driving wasn't fluid.

"When we got to Tan Son Nhut, I was alerted again by the fact that our plane was so far away from the main traffic," she continued. "Finally, when he parked out of sight of the runway, I reached into my bag. After that, it was obvious that he was going to kill us.

"He walked around the front of the car, past you to get to the bags in the back seat, instead of going the short way. I was pretending to look over the fence, but he couldn't see where my eyes were, and once he withdrew his pistol, and began to raise it, I fired."

She put out her cigarette and reached for another.

"I'm sorry I shot your friend," she said, but showed no emotion.

I said nothing but thought about what she said. It was perfectly consistent with what I had seen. It was simple; no elaboration, improbable coincidences, or anything that required imagination.

"Who was he aiming at?"

"I didn't wait to find out," the countess said.

"Do you think he was going to kill both of us?" I asked.

"Yes."

She lit her second cigarette, but didn't repeat the deep inhalation she had done with the first one.

"Actually," she resumed, "I'm not sure he was going to kill us both. I *am* sure he was going to kill me."

This gave me a chill. I took a deep breath and said what had been on my mind since I heard the shot.

"I thought you were going to kill me next," I said.

For a second, I thought she was going to laugh, but then looked crushed.

"I could never do that, Bill," she said, her eyes glistening. "Never," she repeated in a whisper.

I looked into her eyes, trying to fathom her truthfulness;

her thoughts; the way she understood what was unfolding.

"Why would anyone want you dead?" I asked.

"I know too much; I've done too many things," she said, pre-empting my next question. "It would be easier for a lot of people if I did not survive this war. After Borroughs killed me, if he thought you'd make trouble, he would have killed you, too."

"Oh, I would have made trouble," I said, deep anger taking hold.

She put the hand not holding the cigarette on mine.

"I know you would," she said. "I'm glad it didn't come to that."

We sat quietly, almost trusting each other.

"What I don't understand is, Borroughs' body must have been discovered between the time we took off from Saigon, and the time we landed here: so why haven't we been arrested?" I asked.

She took a long drag, then stubbed out the cigarette.

"I don't know," she said, very quietly.

"All I can think is that Borroughs was working for someone else. The Viet Cong? The North Vietnamese? The Khmer Rouge?"

"I think it more likely to be a contract killing," the countess said.

"What do you mean? Contracted by whom?"

The suggestion surprised me. In a war, you expect enemies, factions, underground groups; you don't expect contract killers. I felt the countess had a good deal more to tell.

"If the American or British governments wanted either of us dead, they would have taken us away, not killed us in plain sight," I said. "That means Borroughs must have been working either for the enemy, or some other group."

"There is another possibility," the countess said.

"Yes?"

"That we die here," she said. "There's still more than an hour before we get on the plane."

Chapter XVII

If that was going to happen, it would be easy to do it in the controlled environment of the air base, or the open areas of the commercial terminal. Either way, my illusion of safety had been banished, and I would not feel safe until I was airborne, or in Calcutta, or *en route* to the place after that.

Borroughs a hit man? I still rejected it, but if it came down to a choice between him and the countess – no, that wasn't straight-forward, either.

The countess was probably having similar thoughts as she stared out the window on to a parking area for service vehicles.

"Countess, will you give me your pistol?" I asked.

"You don't trust me, Bill?" she asked, almost pathetically.

"I can't be seen to trust you," I said. "You killed a member of the US Army. I might be helping you to escape, but I should at least be able to claim I disarmed you."

It sounded as silly to her as it did to me, and she actually laughed.

She passed her bag over to me.

"All right. I'll accept that explanation, but I'll let you take it out, lest you duck when I do."

I opened the bag, and took out the small piece, slipped out the clip and cleared the chamber. I put the clip in one pocket and the Beretta in the other, and slid the bag back to her.

"I suppose you should start calling me 'Françoise'," the countess said. "I will have to get used to it, and 'Countess' attracts too much attention. It didn't matter in Saigon, but anywhere else, it could lead to awkward questions."

I nodded.

"That will take some getting used to," I said. "I'm used to thinking of you as 'Countess'."

"What will happen to you?" she asked. "Will you have to go to the Ministry in London for debriefing?"

"It wouldn't surprise me if you did, too," I said.

She shook her head.

"I would be so unwelcome there."

"I wish I knew why," I said.

"You deserve to know," she said. "I will tell you everything once we pass the point of no return on the way to Calcutta."

I glanced at my watch. There was just under an hour until our flight.

"Come along, Countess," I said. "Time to go."

We walked back to the Air Force building and met Sergeant Pacelli.

"Perfect, sir," he said, glancing at the clock. "I'll take you over to TWA, and help you check in."

He pushed a dolly with our suitcases as we walked nearly a quarter of a mile to the passenger terminal. We passed through a security point, but my orders and Françoise's passport were enough to get us through.

"This flight only goes a few times a week, so your timing is good," Pacelli said.

We weren't travelling first class, nor yet business, but the sergeant led us to the priority desk where he seemed to know the agent.

"Major Murdock's compliments, and could you please extend every possible courtesy to Lieutenant Bradley and Miss Mauriac," he said.

"Of course, Tony," the agent replied, and giggled. "Sorry, Sergeant Pacelli."

Our bags were taken, and we were told that boarding would begin in five minutes.

"The airline schedules in this part of the world are more

suggestions than commitments," Pacelli said, when we were out of range of his girlfriend. "Major Murdock says that you will be met in Calcutta by a British Royal Navy officer who will give you your new orders, and advise you of your onward travel arrangements. Good luck, sir; Miss Mauriac."

Sergeant Pacelli saluted me, and as I had my cover on, I returned his salute.

୫

"I'm so glad you're with me," the countess said when we were strapped in.

The 707 was about two thirds full. The seats were arranged three-and-two; we had a two. The countess was by the window and had held my hand since sitting down. The look of self-possessed control was gone; she just looked young, uncertain, and tired.

We took off more or less on time, and we reclined our seats, and she leaned against me and slept.

I had so little idea about her life, or what she'd been doing for Hawthorne. What I did know – or at least believed – was that she'd probably saved my life. I also knew that she had killed a man this morning, and seemed extraordinarily calm about it. With my right hand, I tapped my pocket just to ensure that the Beretta was there.

The flight to Calcutta was just under three hours, so I

made a mental note to wake the countess in one-and-a-half hours, and see if she'd "tell me everything."

The comfort and smoothness of the flight had me dozing, and when I woke, there was less than an hour left before we arrived.

I gently nudged the countess, and she immediately opened her eyes.

"I woke up a few minutes ago," she said, sitting up.

I turned in my seat so I faced her. Anyone seeing us would think we were lovers, absorbed in each other. Without me saying a word, the countess nodded, and began.

"Please don't hate me," she began. "You and I have been caught up in some serious business. You had the easier job, delivering messages; I had to carry out the instructions.

"My father was – is – an adventurer. He was born in India, which makes him British. He was cashiered from the army in his early twenties – the usual thing, disappearing mess funds. A cliché, but for good reason. After the army, he worked around India and Southeast Asia doing all sorts of things. He was a mercenary, an arms dealer, a smuggler of all sorts of goods, but never knowingly drugs or people – though he did help a number of people escape from unfriendly forces. He rescued someone who had been kidnapped in a clandestine British Army operation.

"I learned some of this from my mother, and other bits he told me himself when I was older. Apart from those criminal activities, he was surprisingly honest," she said with an ironic laugh.

"He was in and out of jail, but was one of those great characters who with a combination of guile and charm, could get out of most things. Dress him in a business suit or dinner jacket, and he could get into the board room of the Bank of England, or the Carlton Club – I think he did that, actually.

"To my mother and me, he was very kind, very generous, and a lot of fun. My mother told me that she believed he was absolutely faithful to her. I've heard nothing to make me disbelieve that," she said.

While there was obviously some pain in these memories, they were equally obviously very good ones. Her voice indicated love and forgiveness.

"This has little to do with you, but it is how I became involved. A few years ago, my father was captured by a less than friendly government, and became a negotiation pawn involving the British government," she explained. "Someone found out about my existence, and the Foreign Office, and MI7 determined that my location in Saigon might be useful.

"I was told that if I carried out various jobs for the British, they would work to free my father. Considering he had been a thorn in their paw for long time, they pointed out, it was very generous on their part. Of course, I complied. I had no idea what I was agreeing to, but I wanted my father's freedom."

"Of course," I said.

She looked at me as if to see whether I was really buying this story.

"It began with delivering alleged propaganda scripts, just as you did."

"There were real scripts?" I asked.

I had long suspected that there never were, but didn't want to know what I might really be doing.

"One or two," she said. "Once they trusted me, the real messages began."

She paused.

"This is where it gets hard," she said, and her tone frightened me.

"As you can imagine, there was a lot of British wealth in Vietnam. Even though it was a French colony, there were significant business interests, and ways needed to be found to get money, financial instruments, and other documents, and quantities of precious metals out of the country.

"You and I were part of the chain that enabled that to happen," she said. "It involved a network of British expats and sympathisers as well as some contract operatives."

"Contract operatives?" I asked, fearing what the euphemism might conceal.

"Burglars. Thieves. The odd armed robber. People who could disguise crates, and get them on ships."

Protecting wealth and property is instinctive, and governments – especially governments in crisis – create impediments to exercising this instinct.

"Why would the British government be interested in helping these people?" I asked.

She smiled, and nodded.

"Exactly what I wanted to know," she said. "No one told me directly, but I think I worked it out: at the most obvious, the government, and individual companies didn't want millions of pounds of bearer bonds, cash, gold, or precious stones to fall into the hands of the communists. Secondly, disclosure of who was involved in what, could embarrass some very highly placed people; possibly even destabilise the government."

"What could do that?" I asked, thinking that the countess' imagination had strayed too much into Ian Fleming territory.

"Behind some of these companies, there are men who are ruthless," she said. "Men who blackmail, bribe, hire thugs, and killers to protect their wealth, but apart from the bribes, kick-backs, and contracts, there is something else that is even more dangerous for the politicians," she said.

"What's that?"

"Disclosure of the financial and material assistance that Britain is – or at least was – clandestinely giving to the Republic of South Vietnam."

It took a moment to absorb this.

"*Are you serious?*" I asked.

If true, this was dynamite. It would reveal the hypocrisy and deception of successive governments. Fortunes, reputations, knighthoods, and seats in the House of Lords were at stake.

She nodded.

"No wonder you're in fear of your life."

All this demonstrated my almost total *naiveté*, and I began to understand why Europeans spoke to Americans the way they did, and even then, we didn't get it.

One might argue that the financial moguls, tax evaders, traders and smugglers had dubious rights to their treasures, it was also clear that an invading communist force had none. As for the duplicitous politicians, well, they had always existed. Their aid will not have been unknown to the American government, which is probably why they agreed to the involvement of my predecessors and me.

While I was not a believer in the "I was just following orders" defence, I think this was still in the realm of what a reasonably prudent person would do, though I couldn't completely absolve myself of Borroughs' death.

I had once been told that if you find yourself employing the sort of reasoning I was currently using, you should bail out and start running. I was just too innocent to have the sense to do that, which, of course, was why I had been chosen.

The stewardess announced the beginning of our descent into Calcutta, so we stowed our trays, opened the blinds, fastened our seatbelts, and put our seats in the upright position.

I settled back and closed my eyes. The countess had been brave, and served Britain well. She had also saved my life. As far as I could see, there was no reason to hate her. Quite the contrary.

"Bill," she said, pulling on my arm. "I'm not finished."

I put my hand gently on hers and squeezed it, as if to say, I didn't need to know any more.

"The British are meeting this plane," she said.

Her voice was urgent.

"Even though I was working for them, they have reason to want me out of the way," she said.

"Out of the way? Exile out of the way, or dead out of the way?"

"I don't think it matters," she said.

This melodramatic expression made me laugh.

"No one's going to harm you," I said. "It's 1973: the British and the Americans are reasonably civilised."

Her faced reddened with frustration.

"Will you *listen* to me!" she explained in a burst of exasperation.

She was breathing hard, and I thought she was about to explode again, when the plane banked steeply, and she grabbed my arm, before laughing at her own reaction.

"Please," she said softly. "It's important."

I moved away from her to see her better, and turned in my seat as much as possible.

"You remember that part of my work was working with the chef?"

I nodded.

"He used to do catering jobs for important people, and I'd

work in the kitchen, or sometimes wait on tables. I saw international businessmen, corporation executives, shipping magnates, bankers, and government officials, and lots of high-ranking military officers.

"The food was beautiful, and the old French wines would appear. I would serve, and pour, and I was perfectly placed to carry out special instructions from MI7."

She had set the scene well, and I didn't like what plot it suggested.

"On orders, delivered by you and your predecessors, the odd individual would receive a food additive. There were different ones," she said. "Some were supplied, others, I made myself, with ingredients to complement the food or wine being served."

I looked at her. Her face displayed no regret, except that she had to disillusion me.

"So, you see, dear Lieutenant Bradley," she said very gently, "that is why the British would like me out of the way."

Chapter XVIII

Although I had not fully digested what the countess had told me, I held her hand as the plane descended. I wasn't going to cut her loose until I knew more, and while I thought she deserved protection, I didn't know how far I would go.

She remained quiet as the plane landed and taxied to the terminal. We were about a third of the way back, and exited normally when the aisle cleared. While more humid, Calcutta was slightly cooler than Saigon and Bangkok, but was still around eighty.

We passed easily through immigration, and waited to collect our bags. I put them on a trolley, and we pushed through the doors to the outside world.

Still dressed in her white *áo dài*, the countess would be instantly recognised. On the plus side, a Royal Navy uniform would be obvious, too.

I suspected the countess didn't want to look, but I spotted the uniform a few seconds before the lieutenant saw us. I pushed the trolley around the barrier and approached him. We saluted each other.

"Lieutenant Bradley, Miss Mauriac," he said. "Geoffrey Rodgers. Attaché to the British Consul's office. "Welcome to Calcutta, though I have to tell you that you will not be here long enough to enjoy it fully."

I sensed the countess tense.

We shook hands.

"You must be tired," he said to the countess. "Early start, flights, and different time zones. It's noontime here. Are you ravenous?"

We moved to the front door where the traffic was incredible, where vehicles of every kind waited, tried to get in, move away or wait. Horns, bells and buzzers sounded in an overpowering cacophony.

Lieutenant Rodgers took the countess' suitcase from the trolley, and I took mine. We followed him through the traffic to a traffic island where an official car waited. An Indian driver opened the door for us. The countess and I sat in the back seat, and Rodgers sat in the jump seat facing us.

"I've got good news and bad news," the lieutenant said.

When he saw the countess look worried, he quickly corrected himself.

"Not really bad news, Miss, Mauriac, but, let's say, inconvenient," he said smiling, but not succeeding in getting one in return. "The good news is that I'm taking you to a hotel where you can eat, sleep, wash, change or do whatever you like for a few hours.

"The so-called bad news is that you have one more flight today. I'll collect you at five o'clock this afternoon, and take you to the airport. There is a six-thirty flight to Bombay, where you will spend the night."

"How long is that flight?" the countess asked.

"Just under three hours."

"That's about the same as Bangkok to here," I said.

"Is it? I've never done it," Lieutenant Rodgers said. "You will be met by another attaché like me."

The countess sat back, and leaned her head against my shoulder as we lurched along. Rodgers and I spoke of a few neutral things, until he announced that we were nearly at the hotel.

The countess sat up and looked about.

"It's called the Grand Hotel," Rodgers explained. "Whether it is or not, you can decide, but curiously, it gets its name from a Colonel Grand whose house used to occupy the land."

"That's not true!" the countess exclaimed with a laugh and a big smile.

"I swear to you, it is, Miss Mauriac," he said. "The consulate keeps a suite here – has done since before Indian independence – so enjoy it as much as you can."

The driver carried our bags in, and Lieutenant Rodgers stayed with us until we'd registered.

"I will see you down here at five o'clock," he said. "You may prefer to travel in civilian clothes, if you've got any."

"Thank you, Lieutenant," the countess said.

The suite comprised two large bedrooms, each with a bath and balcony, and a large sitting room, also with a balcony with views over a park. On a dining table was a large assortment of food and bottled drinks.

"I'm going to have a bath," the countess announced. "Then a comfortable nap, and a change of clothes. Unfortunately, I don't have much to choose from."

I thought of Rodger's remark; if only I had some civilian clothes, I'd be in them instantly. As it was, I took off my shoes, socks and tie, collected a plateful of food, and stretched out on the long sofa. About an hour later, I had a shower and put on clean clothes.

The countess emerged from her room at just after four. I hardly recognised her.

She was wearing a knee-length skirt, and a white cotton short-sleeved shirt with a scooped neckline. Her hair was tied in a ponytail which brushed her shoulders when she turned her head. With her make-up, she looked like an advertisement in *Paris Match*. She wore low-heeled light brown shoes, but as I had only seen her wear the traditional flat rubber-soled cloth shoes, these gave her additional height.

"What have you done with the countess?" I asked, but even now she was wearing the gold chain I'd given her.

"I'm feeling much better," she said, and sat next to me.

"Thank you," she said.

"What for?"

"For staying with me," she said.

"I'm just following orders," I said, then added, "And I am very happy to do so."

She looked at me for a moment.

"I want you to trust me the way I trust you," she said. "Of all the other Navy officers I worked with – and some were very nice – I never felt as safe with any of them as I do with you. And – "

"You *did* save my life – God! Was that only this morning?"

"We're flying West, and the day is getting longer," the countess said.

"Are you all ready to leave?" I asked.

"Yes. It was good to relax for a while."

"And, do you feel safer?"

"I think I am safe until we get to the final destination," she replied. "After that, who knows? A disappearance, or jail? I suppose I could be handed over to the Americans."

"I don't think they would have brought you all the way back just to shoot you on British soil," I said. "Also, my orders said I was to accompany you, not guard you. I've not been told not to let you escape."

"Well, they are not bringing me back to give me a bungalow in Surrey."

I put my arm around her, not knowing how she might react. She leaned comfortably into me, resting her head on my chest.

"*Je veux juste que ce soit terminé.* I just want this to be over," she said to herself quietly.

We sat like that for ten minutes, barely speaking. When it was time to go, we left the suite wordlessly, and went to meet Lieutenant Rodgers.

He was in the lobby when we arrived, and his expression when he saw the countess made us both laugh.

"Blimey!" he blurted before recovering himself. "I beg your pardon, Miss Mauriac, but that's quite a transformation."

"I don't have to play Katisha anymore," she said.

"Wrong country," I said.

"But right character."

The Indian driver took our cases to the car. When we were in, and had turned into the traffic, Lieutenant Rodgers spoke.

"The consul and I hope you were able to have some rest and relax."

The countess thanked him for the hospitality.

"I don't know where you're going after Bombay, but I wish you safe travels," he said, as the car suddenly braked.

There were angry words outside the car in Hindi or Bengali, but our driver was silent.

"One of the good things about India is there is no rush hour," Rodgers said. "The streets are congested *all* the time."

It was amusing to see how he looked at the countess. He wasn't leering, but simply fascinated by her transformation. He'd go from looking at her, to looking out the window, but kept being drawn back to her face. She surreptitiously gave my hand a squeeze, and I knew she was trying not to laugh.

"With any luck, you should be at your hotel nine-thirty Bombay time," he said.

He then turned to me.

"Were you on Yankee Station?"

"For eight months. I'm a fully-fledged member of the Gulf of Tonkin Yacht Club."

I told him about the cruisers I was on. He probably knew, but as a naval man, he'd be interested. I told him about the different carriers I'd landed on.

"What's next for you? Do you know?" he asked.

"Probably a court martial," I said.

The countess turned quickly to look at me, while Rodgers looked embarrassed.

"What for?" he burbled, then tried to retract the question.

"Transporting a minor over several international borders," I said.

There was a second's silence, then the countess laughed.

"I'm not a minor! I'm over twenty-one," she said.

"Good girl," I said. "Keep saying that. Someone might believe you."

When Rodgers overcame being dumbfounded, he joined our laughter.

"I don't know what I'm doing next. With all the cuts in personnel, I expect that I'll get my papers and go back to the States and sell shoes, or something."

Rodgers asked a few more innocuous questions of me, but didn't dare ask the countess anything.

When we got to the airport, he accompanied us to check-in, and saw us move through to the gate.

"Still feeling refreshed?" I asked the countess.

"For the moment," she said. "Three flights in one day is too many. Wouldn't it be nice if we had a hotel like that tonight?"

Our Air India flight to Bombay was another 707, and, again we had the pair of seats. The countess didn't seem to mind flying, at least she didn't comment on it.

"What is going on in your head?" she asked me after we took off.

"Oh, lots of things; it's a jumble," I said. "Some quite nice, others not so much."

"I bet what you are dreaming about is just what you said to Lieutenant Rodgers: being back home, leading a normal life with no war, no military, and no countess. What do you like doing in your spare time? Do you hunt? Fish? Play baseball, or golf? I know you like reading, and seeing films; what do you want your life to be like?"

It was like watching the metamorphosis of an animal. A spontaneity was emerging; a genuine young lady who I could imagine staying up late dancing, or talking with friends; smoking and drinking white wine.

"After all you've experienced, and from the bits we've shared, I don't think there's a lot of difference in what we want," I said.

"*Peut-être*."

She reclined her seat and put her pillow on my shoulder.

I woke her when we began our descent. We couldn't see anything, and I could tell she was becoming anxious about who would be meeting us, and where we might be taken.

We were met by another Royal Navy lieutenant. John Bowker was also an attaché in the local consul's office. He, too, had a driver and similar official car.

"I'm sorry," the countess said, after he had introduced himself. "It's been a very long day, I am not very good company."

"Miss Mauriac, I am not here to be entertained," he replied easily. "Serbjit and I are going to take you to a hotel near the Fort, about half an hour from here, where I hope you will be very comfortable. I will give Lieutenant Bradley the necessary papers, and he can go over them with you in the morning.

"You can have a civilised start to the day. I'll collect you at ten o'clock for an eleven-thirty flight to Cairo," he said.

We both woke up suddenly. Why would we be going to Cairo? As far as I knew, the US didn't have diplomatic relations with Egypt. I could feel the countess' body react on the seat next to me. I glanced at her face, but it didn't register any-thing.

"Cairo? That's interesting," I said. "We're on a magical mystery tour that today has taken us from Saigon to Bangkok, to Calcutta to here – and tomorrow, Cairo."

"Where are you hoping this will take you?" he asked.

"Miss Mauriac is *en route* back to Toulouse," I said. "But I have no idea where my next assignment will be."

The countess didn't want to be in this conversation, and was looking out the window. I explained about the probability of getting a cut, which was uninteresting enough to pass the time safely.

We arrived at the Grand Hotel (this one not named after Colonel Grand), which from the outside looked like it could be in Kensington. Understated, perhaps even sedate, it had the ambience of a London club. The countess perked up when she saw it.

When we checked in, Lieutenant Bowker, who had spent the last ten minutes telling me how anxious he was to get back to sea, gave me an envelope with our tickets and next instructions.

We had two rooms overlooking a tree-lined boulevard. Within a minute of entering my room, the countess knocked on the adjoining door. I unlocked it and let her in. I knew she wanted to see our instructions.

I opened them, and held them so we could both read. It was just as Bowker had said, we were to fly to Cairo and await further instructions.

"How long is the flight to Cairo?" the countess asked.

I looked at the tickets.

"Six hours."

She sighed, said good-night and went back to her room. She returned a moment later.

"Is it all right if we leave this door open?"

I wanted to reply, "If you feel safe," but said, "If it will make you feel safer."

We had been shown a restaurant downstairs, but we were more tired than hungry, and said good-night again, and went to our beds. The countess' light was out when I switched mine off.

Three flights. Three countries. Two hotels. One murder. I doubted I'd have another day like it.

の

I think it was because there was too much to think about that I could just shut down and sleep. I did fleetingly wonder if leaving the door open had been a good idea, for while I wanted the countess to feel safe, I wanted to feel safe, too. The sight of Borroughs' body, disturbing enough, kept raising the question, "Were we ever supposed to leave Saigon alive?"

In spite of those thoughts, the heat, and the noise from the docks, sleep did come quickly. I was dreaming about fishing, and had actually caught something and was trying to land it, when the thrashings of the fish translated into my arm being shaken.

Immediately awake, I sat up to find the countess sitting on my bed. My start made her jump back.

"What is it?" I asked.

She looked at me not fully daring to say anything.

"Can you, will you, hold me like you did this afternoon?"

I slid back down on the bed and moved over to give her room. I lay back and put an arm around her shoulder, and she rested her head on me. They were the only points where we were touching, it was too hot to lie more closely. Her hair smelled of tea-tree oil, and I idly twisted the ends around my finger as her breathing slowed.

I don't think I moved from that position, for several hours later when I again felt I was being shaken, I was in the same position. It was still dark, but I could feel the countess moving erratically. I put my hand back on her shoulder, and she immediately began sobbing audibly. I said nothing, but held her, and stroked her hair. She was fully awake, and glanced up at me, before closing her eyes.

Minutes went by without her stopping. I was about to try to quiet her before she became hysterical, but it suddenly subsided and she drifted back to sleep. While I felt profoundly sorry for her, it also crossed my mind that whoever took on this lady would have to be prepared for anything.

Chapter XIX

The countess was in her room when I woke up some-time after seven. I showered, shaved, and dressed, trying to look as little crumpled as possible. I still had the Beretta and clip in my pockets.

"Good morning, Bill," the countess said, coming into my room at seven-thirty. "Are you ready for breakfast?"

She was wearing the same skirt, but a different top. Her hair was still in a ponytail, but tied further up the back of her head. She later explained that this was a "high pony-tail," and she thought it wouldn't hit the back of the seat on the plane as much as it had the day before. She was also wearing her gold chain; I didn't know which symbol charm she was wearing, or if it had any special signifi-cance.

We went down to the dining room. She didn't say any-thing in the elevator, and felt distant, as she had done in the first weeks I knew her.

"Who knows when we'll eat again," I said as we lined up for the buffet.

She ate well, and talked about the traffic outside, the ships we could see, and asked me about living on a ship.

"It will be curious if I get to a country that has real seasons where the temperature goes below twenty-seven degrees," she said. "Eighty to you."

"It's the humidity that I don't like," I said. "Working on a ship, it's all air conditioned: cooled and moisture balanced. It makes a big difference to the ability to work. I don't know how people do it here, or Southeast Asia."

"How do you think they'd cope with your Midwestern winters?" she laughed.

It was reassuring to see something of her normal manner, but I was a long way from being used to seeing her dressed as a Westerner.

"Do you want another coffee?" she asked me, holding the pot.

While distant, her manner was more relaxed, which considering the upheaval of her life in the last few days spoke of great internal resources and character. Not many twenty-six-year olds can start the day leaving her home forever, shooting a US soldier, and flying thousands of miles to who knew where with a relative stranger.

The countess ate several helpings of various fresh and dried fruit, while I confined myself to the relative safety of the croissants laid on for the Europeans.

We talked easily about nothing until after nine when we went up to prepare to leave.

"I wish we had time to see some things," she said. "It's a shame just to sleep through these cities."

"I wonder how many more there are," I said.

"I'd like to do some shopping, but there's no point until I know what sort of clothes I should get," she said. "Wool, cotton or silk? Or, will I just have a prison uniform, or a blindfold?"

∞

The next stage of our travels – "travels" was a nicer word than "escape" – went smoothly. While the countess may have been resigned to her fate, I was not. The worst thing I had done was fail to report a murder, which may not have been murder after all, but manslaughter, or better, self-defence. I had not been an assassin for the Ministry of Defence, but, then, the countess had been blackmailed into working for them in the first place.

This wasn't in the spy films: the fact that once you were playing in that murky world (*this* murky world), nothing was ever normal again. The crimes and misdemeanours were buried and papered over, obscured by jargon; but, no one ever forgot, and there was no absolution.

Lieutenant Bowker and Serbjit were prompt and drove us to the airport, and saw us to the gate.

"I wonder how many times they've done this sort of thing before," I said.

"I'd like to think they'd never done it before," the countess replied. "I like thinking that I'm special."

It was the first bit of personal humour she'd expressed that day. I wondered if it was because the threat of Bowker and Serbjit arresting her, or shooting her, had passed.

"Do you play cards?" she asked me.

She was looking in a shop that sold books, magazines and other pastimes for flights.

"Yes."

She went in while I watched planes being moved around the tarmac. Only when she was walking back to me did I wonder what she'd used for money. I didn't have any rupees. I had less than two hundred American dollars, and some Vietnamese notes.

She waved the pack at me.

"Prepare to lose your fortune," she said.

"Can't we just play strip-poker?" I asked.

She laughed.

242

"Wouldn't that be a good scene in a film!" she exclaimed. "It wouldn't be the main focus, but just going on in the background – actually, it would be better on a train where you have four people at a table."

In the time we had before boarding, we walked the length of the terminal, as for the next six hours, we'd hardly be able to move.

It was an Air India flight on one of the new 747s which had come into service two years earlier. Neither of us had been on one, and the enormity compared to the 707s was impressive, if challenging. We had two seats by the window, and would be as comfortable as possible.

While the flight seemed endless, it was punctuated with the usual combination of drinks, meals, duty free sales, and the movie, a Bollywood extravaganza, that we passed on.

Neither of us had anything to read, and had exhausted the airline magazine before we took off. The countess didn't seem to be in the mood for talking, but she opened the cards and began shuffling them.

"What would you like to play?"

We named several games without finding one in common, until she described the one I knew as "gin," so we played that. We agreed on one French Franc per point. Fortunately, when she won the first game, I was only down seven points. I won the second game, but only by five.

It was then lunch time, and following the duty-free sales, and one or two other interruptions, we tried to get some sleep. While the countess settled quickly, I kept opening my eyes to see what was going on in the movie. With no sound, it was tempting to make up dialogue.

It was disconcerting to have so little to think about. I had no work to do, no apartment or house to look after, no decisions to make. The countess and I had both been busy people, and no doubt she identified with what she did as much as I did. While this state of limbo would not last, it was curious that it wasn't more pleasurable. I teased the reason for this for a while before drifting off.

The countess, while she had acted distant, had resumed her now familiar position, holding my arm and supporting the pillow on me.

She slept quietly until we began our approach into Cairo. We landed at five-thirty our time, two o'clock Cairo time. We passed easily through immigration, and collected our suitcases.

I was looking for another naval officer, but saw a US Army captain watching the arriving passengers. He caught my eye and nodded.

"Captain Ian Mackenzie," he said, saluting when we were

close enough to speak.

I returned the salute, which should have been mine to initiate, but he didn't seem bothered.

We moved away from the river of arrivals, and he looked around, and waved to a corporal who had been standing further back.

"Lieutenant Bradley, Miss Mauriac, this is Corporal Stiegman. We are unofficial advisors, which means we're not actually in Egypt," Captain Mackenzie said. "Things are improving here, but are not *normalised* yet."

Salutes were exchanged again. Stiegman took the baggage trolley from me, and headed towards the exit.

"If you would like to stop to freshen up, please do so. We've got a two-hour drive to the hotel," Mackenzie said.

The countess pulled my arm and whispered to me.

"Where are they taking us?"

"Two hours?" I queried.

"Bit of a treat," Mackenzie said. "The British maintain a suite which isn't being used. We don't have such things anymore."

The countess pulled my sleeve again.

"And where is this, Captain?" I asked.

"Alexandria. You'll have a sea view."

While the Cairo traffic was slow, smelly and hot, the journey was worth it when we saw the Mediterranean open before us. The Cecil Hotel was an opulent creation of the 1920s, and resembled one of the more fanciful picture palaces of the Ebersons.

The identical nature of the process of meeting us, accompanying us to hotel registration desks or airport gates, indicated Hawthorne's hand in issuing detailed instructions to all concerned. The fact that all our hotels so far had been arranged by the British supported that inference, as did the precision of the timing that Captain Mackenzie produced the envelope with our instructions.

"If you can be ready at eight o'clock tomorrow morning, we can get you to your eleven o'clock flight in plenty of time," he said. "You may like to go for a walk. It's safe around here, at least during daylight. I wouldn't wear your uniform," he added.

Our suite, while not the size of our rooms in Bombay, was still spacious. Located on a corner of the hotel, the corner room was a sitting room, off which, in opposite directions, were two bedrooms with bathrooms. The windows had balconettes with French windows, and a refreshing, if warm, breeze circulated throughout.

The countess had a shower while I called to see about getting my shirts washed, and a pair of my trousers pressed.

Even though I was travelling in the serviceable khaki service uniform, the hours sitting on planes took their toll. Since I had only the one case and all my uniforms, I had a limited selection of what I could wear. At some stage I'd need to get some civilian clothes, as I knew uniforms were not permitted in France or the UK, and I suspected we were headed that way.

I opened the orders. We were to fly to Athens, where we would be met by another representative from the US Army. There was no indication of what would come next.

Why Athens? If we were headed to London, why were we here? There were plenty of direct flights from Bombay to London. The only conclusion was that we weren't going to London, but why and where was a different matter.

I was wearing an unauthorised combination of khaki trousers with a tropical white short sleeved shirt when the countess came into the sitting room. She was wrapped in a fluffy hotel bathrobe but also wearing the trousers to her *áo dài*.

She burst out laughing when she saw me.

"No matter what, when we get to Athens, we need to get some more clothes," she said. "We're looking ridiculous!"

I agreed, and said there was a good BX there, and we should insist on getting to it, unless they were putting us on another plane right away.

She sat in the opposite corner of the sofa to me.

"Bill, would you mind if I went for a walk? Alone?" she asked. "I'd like the exercise, and I'd like to be on my own for a while."

"I may temporarily be your escort, but I am not your jailer, Countess," I said. "Anyway, I can't go out without civvies, which I have not got."

"You really have no other clothes?"

I shook my head.

She stood.

"Then, I will see you later," she said.

"Be careful, Countess, and please be back by dark. Seriously. I don't want to spend half the night looking for you."

She went into her bedroom, and soon emerged with a brightly coloured top, and a leather bag on a long strap.

"Have you got any money?" I asked, just as she got to the door.

"I have some French francs, a few dollars, and a little sterling, but not enough for a get-away," she said with a laugh, and left.

There was very little for me to do. I wrote up the day's

events in my journal, and hoped I hadn't made a big mistake in letting the countess go out. There was no reason not to trust her. I also re-read our instructions and my orders in the hopes that in the light of where we had been and where we were going tomorrow, that I might discern a plan. Once we were in Western Europe, I was sure that we were in the endgame.

I moved a chair toward the window, and looked out and watched the light change and dim into dusk.

I put on my last clean service khaki shirt (until the laundry came back) for dinner, and was in the process of touching up the polish on my shoes when I heard the countess return.

"A pity you didn't come," she said. "It was beautiful, and the air was lovely closer to the sea."

"I was told not to," I reminded her.

"Yes, that was a pity. About half way up to the beach I went to, I was sorry you weren't there.

"I found a small beach – not really one I'd want to swim from – and sat and enjoyed the calmness. Occasionally, it would be quiet, too."

"Are you hungry?" I asked her.

"Yes," she said. "And tired. Tonight, can we get a bottle of wine?"

We went down to the dining room, which was quiet, as it was still early for fashionable dining, but having crossed several time zones, we were ready to eat. The menu was extensive with a wide variety of international dishes, most of them French.

I thought the countess would choose one of them, but she selected the set meal, and I did the same. She picked up the wine list and perused it with some care. The wine steward came over when she put it down, and she made the order.

A waiter came and removed the superfluous glasses.

Although casually dressed, the countess looked elegant. There was still anxiety in her face when she was quiet and still, but she was cheerful, and chatted easily.

"I think we're getting near the end of our journey," she said. "I think you do, too."

"I was thinking about that while you were out," I said. "I think you're right."

"What makes you think so?" she asked. "I want to see how similar our reasoning is."

She was smiling as she said this, as though we were trying to solve the same puzzle, and test each other's theories. I told her about flying to Athens and not London.

She nodded.

"That's almost what I was thinking," she said. "Only, I was thinking about flights to Paris, of which there are as many as to London. That leaves the question of where the final stop will be."

"I think that you and I have different destinations," I said.

"So do I," she said quietly, "but let's not talk about that until later. Until we have to."

This reply immediately made me want to ask what her reasoning was, and if she was still afraid for her life.

The arrival of the bottle of Bordeaux prevented me from questioning her, and the wine ritual moved on. When the sample was poured, she swirled it, smelled it, and tasted it, doing whatever wine lovers do, sucking in air, and sloshing it about in their mouths. She did this quickly and efficiently, making no show of it, and making it look like something she did every day. Perhaps she did.

She nodded her approval, and our glasses were poured. I was surprised that she didn't take a drink immediately. I was about to propose a toast to her future safety and happiness, but noticed that she was gazing at me. I was startled when I suspected what it meant, but returned her gaze.

When we became self-conscious of our behaviour, I could see her calculating what to say. Eventually, she reached for her glass, and raised it.

"Lieutenant Bradley: thank you," was all she could manage.

We touched glasses, and drank.

The first course arrived shortly afterwards, and the countess began talking about food, and how such dishes were prepared. When she stopped long enough to eat something, I raised my glass.

"Countess, you saved my life. I shall live in your debt."

She was looking at me more seriously than before.

"Although I grew up in the Orient, I do not believe that I am now responsible for your life," she said.

I smiled, then she added:

"At least not in the traditional sense."

Neither of us said anything for a while, then she said, "I think it would be best for us if we talked about something else."

The rest of the meal glided by with superficial talk, excellent food, and a powerful subtext. When we finished, she walked with a cool detachment to the elevator, and we returned to our suite. My clothes had been returned and were hanging in the closet.

After the good meal, the bottle of wine, coffee and brandy, not to mention the day's travel time differences, I was tired. I went in the bedroom and took my shoes off when the countess called.

I went into the sitting room where she was standing. She was still fully dressed but had untied her hair, giving her another different look.

"Aren't you very tired?" I asked her.

She came towards me until she was only a foot away.

"You *can* keep secrets," she said. "You were a good choice for this job. I've done this much, much longer than you, and you're one of the best I've worked with. You know how to keep your mouth shut.

"You've seen things, and I've told you things that others would have reported, but you haven't, Lieutenant Bradley. And, all today, I waited for you to mention last night, and you didn't," she said.

I couldn't tell whether this pleased or displeased her. Perhaps she didn't know, but now, she was every bit the countess: cool, in control, deliberate in every word and movement, and I saw how this lady would be able to kill.

"We may not have another opportunity after tonight," she began, "and I wanted you to know that your honesty, and reliability have meant a lot."

"Reliability?" I almost laughed. Was I being compared to a car?

She gave me her tolerant smile.

"You never missed an appointment, except that time you couldn't get a connection. You would be surprised how many of my contacts would just not bother coming. They'd get as far as the air base, then go swimming for the day, or sit around drinking and playing cards or pool, and I'd wait and have to contact Melville, and start again.

"I know two who even read my instructions. One of them, when he did, came and told me what he thought of me, and Melville had to find someone else. There were only two besides you who were completely reliable. Two in six years."

"What – "

"They're both dead."

She answered my question before I'd finished it. That was becoming a regular occurrence.

"I only killed one of them."

"The reliable ones are dead?" I asked. "What about the unreliable ones?"

"Oh, they're dead, too."

Was this going to be good-bye in the long good-bye sense?

"I'm trying very hard not to let you shock me. Good-night, Countess," I said this gently, and stepped away.

She caught my arm.

"I'm not finished, Lieutenant Bradley," she said softly, and pulled herself to me and kissed me. For a long time.

I hugged her tightly, and enjoyed every fleeting second.

"Good-night, Bill," she said, and went to her room.

I turned out the lights in the sitting room, and returned to my bedroom, and prepared for bed. I'd have to write up the rest of my journal the next day, if I was still around to do it.

The night was hot, but the breeze led me to slip under the sheet. I hadn't had time to fall asleep, when the countess came into the room, lifted the sheet, and climbed in. I put my arm around her, and she lay against me as she had done the previous night.

I was about to say something as I moved closer, but she put a finger to my lips.

"Later," she whispered.

Chapter XX

Later came shortly before five in the morning, and again at about ten to six. We lay together unspeaking for nearly half an hour, watching the sky show hints of lightening.

"We need one good memory from this dirty business," she said, kissing me lightly before getting up.

She said almost nothing as we got ready for the next leg of our journey. There was so little in her body language as we went down to breakfast that suggested she even knew me, that I began to question whether what we had just done meant anything to her. This was, after all, the girl who shot a man, then calmly walked on to an airplane.

We went into the dining room and had a continental breakfast. While not silent, the countess' mind was elsewhere, and conversation was hesitant.

"It's a shame to be in this lovely room for so short a time," I said, when we'd gone back up to collect our bags.

The countess took my hand in the elevator, and seconds before the door opened, leaned against me.

"Please look after me, Bill," she said.

"I'll do all I can."

Captain Mackenzie was waiting for us when the elevator doors opened. Both he and Corporal Steigman were in casual civilian clothes.

"I do wish you had some civvies, Lieutenant," Mackenzie said.

"Can't be helped. No need for them on shipboard," I said. "We've been on the move for four days."

"Well, in three hours, it won't be my problem," Mackenzie said.

"I hope you had a comfortable night," he said.

"And a delicious dinner," the countess replied.

On the ride to the airport, Captain Mackenzie explained the subtlety of the relationship between the Egyptians and the Americans, and how under Sadat, things had much improved. He commented that much of his work with the consulate was like other military assignments: long periods of not much going on, then sudden explosions of activity. Hurry up and wait.

As we drove into the airport, I sensed that we were not going to the passenger terminal. The countess noticeably tensed, no doubt realising that if we were headed to another Borroughs situation, she was no longer armed.

Corporal Stiegman, however, drove in front of a small building with a USAF sign on it, and pulled up near some maintenance vehicles.

"A bit of a treat today," Mackenzie said. "You are being spared cattle class on TWA."

He pointed out the window at an awaiting C-11 Gulfstream II.

"That will take you directly to the US base at Hellenikon, in Athens," he said. "You will be met by my Athenian counterpart."

We thanked him, and walked towards the plane as Stiegman handed our bags to the crew.

While still a private jet, the interior was not kitted out as it is in the films. There were six business class type seats with tables, arranged two and one, and a few rows of tourist class seats three abreast.

The countess took a seat by the window, and I sat next to her.

"Did you bring the cards?" I asked.

A few minutes later, the rest of the crew came aboard along with a pilot who was dead-heading back to Hellenikon, and three men in civilian clothes, who took the tourist seats, but not before having a good look at the countess as they passed. I didn't notice until I turned to her to comment that she had slipped on her dark glasses.

"They're going to think you're a film star," I said.

"No," she said. "They're going to think I am what I am: a spy and an assassin."

It was my only flight in a private jet, and I had never expected the US government to provide it, and this flight had CIA written all over it. The sense of speed and power were unlike anything I'd experienced. Beneath us, the Mediterranean was like a mill pond, and we could see the wakes of dozens of ships of all sizes beneath us. As we descended into Athens, we passed over an American carrier, that even at 20,000 feet looked huge. I made out the number 67 on the bow end of the flight deck and would check its identity when I had the chance.

We touched down easily, and taxied to the small terminal building. As the steps of the plane unfolded, we saw an Air Force Captain and an Army Lieutenant with an airman move purposefully towards us.

"Our welcoming party," I said.

"Three of them," she said.

"In case you shoot one of them," I thought.

We descended to the apron, and I saluted the Air Force Captain who met us. His name was Frankel, and he was an assistant to the base commander. With him was a

Lieutenant Jordan, and a Senior Airman called Norton.

The captain welcomed us to Athens, and led us into the terminal building. The countess bumped my arm, which I took as a substitute for a reassuring touch of my hand. I gave her a slight bump back, and she gave the hint of a smile. No one asked to see our passports or orders. Apart from the commercial flights, no one had since we left Bangkok.

"Your next stage is to Brindisi," Captain Frankel said. "Lieutenant Jordan will accompany you."

He looked at his watch.

"Your ferry leaves at three," he said. "Norton will drive you all to Piraeus. There is time for lunch, if you like."

"What we really need to do is go to the BX and get some clothes. All I have are my uniforms, and Mlle Mauriac also needs some things," I said.

The captain looked at Jordan.

"I don't see that's a problem, sir," he said. "We'd better set off right away, though."

Norton put our suitcases in a staff car, and we set off.

At the exchange, Jordan said something that admitted the countess, while I showed my ID. Given the prices, it was hard not to spend my remaining dollars, but I bought shirts, a pair of Levi's, a pair of chinos, a light windbreaker, and some very cheap, but comfortable docksiders.

I didn't want to intrude on the countess' shopping, but I did offer her money in the event she didn't have enough. I had no idea how much she might have with her.

It took us less than forty minutes to complete our purchases, and a few more to stuff them into our cases before driving to the port.

Norton left us, and we walked through the gate, and boarded the ship, *Eirene*. It was a pretty standard Mediterranean ferry that had seen decades of service. With minimal assistance, we found our staterooms. The countess and I were next to each other towards the bow, while Lieutenant Jordan was further back, in a less superior class.

I dropped my bag in my cabin, and helped the countess put hers on the rack. Both our cabins had portholes and seemed to be well ventilated, though the scent of marine diesel was never far away.

I turned to leave her to unpack, but she pushed the door shut.

"Brindisi?!" she said, incredulously. "Why do they want me in Brindisi?"

"They are spending serious money on you, Countess," I said. "Are they trying to buy your silence?"

She looked angrily at me, but her look softened.

"They know I keep my mouth shut," she said. "I have never told anyone what I have told you, and I only did that because of what you saw. I didn't want you to think – "

"That you'd never done that before?" I thought, but kept quiet.

The countess shook her head.

"I don't know what I didn't want you to think," she said.

"Countess, I've said nothing to you about your future, because I don't know what it is," I began. "What I do know, is that it is going to take you a long time to come to terms with the last few years. You've suffered personal tragedy, and been caught up in what you described as 'this nasty business.' It will also take you time to adjust to your new circumstances, whatever they are. I wish I could tell you it won't be hard, but I'm pretty sure that you'll come through it. Maybe you'll even find some happiness. I hope so."

The look on her face, and the hardness of those pale blue eyes, told me that my speech had not gone down as well as I'd hoped. I put my hands gently on her arms, and she tensed, rigid. Nevertheless, I kissed her gently on her forehead.

"Let me know when you're ready to go on deck and explore the ship. I don't know about you, but I'm starving," I said and closed the door behind me.

I had a wash and changed into my new clothes. I'd picked up two paperbacks at the BX, and started one while waiting for the countess. We weren't due to cast off for another fifteen minutes, and I wanted to be on deck to watch.

About ten minutes later, there was a knock on my door. The countess wore what I assumed was a new top with a taupe skirt, shorter than the one she'd been wearing. Her hair was in a lower ponytail, and she was wearing her dark glasses.

"You look refreshed," I said. "And nice."

"Thank you. It's good to see you in civilian clothes for a change."

It hadn't occurred to me that she hadn't seen me in anything but a uniform. It was curious to dress casually after so long.

We went on deck and found Lieutenant Jordan.

"Ah! You look like real human beings now," he said. "How long have you been travelling?"

The countess gave an abbreviated account. I deliberately left it to her, as I didn't want to reveal more than she wanted. It seemed to satisfy Jordan, whose next questions were about the nature of Air India, travelling on a 747, and what the Gulfstream was like.

We were standing on the starboard side watching the shore detail cast off, and amid a cloud of black smoke, the boat began moving away from the pier. It was only fifteen minutes late.

We stayed on deck until we were a mile or so out to sea, then went inside for a meal. We had kebabs and salad, and Lieutenant Jordan introduced us to the delights of retsina. Used to French wines, the countess couldn't believe she was drinking turpentine.

"All of my ancestors are rolling in their graves," she exclaimed. "I may never taste anything again!"

She laughed easily, and continued to drink it. It was cold and refreshing, and offered a further proof that we were now a long way from Saigon.

After lunch, the countess went to sit in the sun, and Jordan and I made our way slowly around the deck. He was curious about what we were doing, as he'd never seen anyone take this route back to France before.

"I can't tell you much, except Mlle Mauriac is someone the Americans wanted to get out of Saigon quickly and safely, and they didn't want her followed. I haven't been read into any more than that. I'm just a public affairs officer," I said.

Jordan nodded.

"I have seen cases like that, but usually they fly them out," he said.

"It wasn't my decision. I'm sorry if we've messed up your week."

"Hey, this is great!" he said. "I'm out of the office, I can sit in the sun, and have a decent meal or two that I'll get reimbursed for, and I've got a Mediterranean cruise."

"Will you return by ship?" I asked.

"I'll hand Miss Mauriac and you over to whoever meets us in Brindisi, and I'll come back on this ship. There are no regular military flights out of Brindisi, and they sure as hell aren't going to lay on a Gulfstream for me!"

❧

As an old, working ferry the *Eirene*'s furnishings were basic. While there were large expanses of open deck, seating was limited to rows of wooden benches, or long benches along the bulkheads. The three of us were seated on small, facing benches on the port side towards the stern. I read my book, while Lieutenant Jordan tried to make polite conversation with the countess.

He asked about her time in Saigon, how long she'd been there, what she was writing about, what her views as a French person were about the way things had turned out.

Between his questions, she asked him about his work;

famous people he might have seen; places he had visited; and similar things to those he asked her. He was circumspect about talking about the colonels.

The countess kept up her cover very well, giving the minimum of concrete information. She cleverly took the initiative and spoke about daily life, shopping for food, learning to cook Vietnamese dishes, and cycling in traffic. She told him about wearing an *áo dài*, and *nón lá*, and learning to soak it.

I recognised many of the things she had told me, and Jordan was as fascinated as I had been. Confident that she was in control, I tuned them out and focused on my reading until it was time for dinner.

Food arrangements were not sophisticated. We waited in a cafeteria line and collected salads, bread, wine, and desserts, and ordered the hot food, which was brought to us when it was ready.

Lieutenant Jordan had money to cover our expenses, though he wasn't certain where it came from. He had enough to buy coffees and several Metaxas after dinner. We remained in the cafeteria to drink them, as it was now dark outside, and Jordan didn't want to risk being overheard.

It wasn't late when the countess and I pleaded tiredness from our repeated early starts and time zone changes, said good-night and went to our cabins.

Well, not exactly; the countess followed me into mine, but left the door open. Her cabin and mine were mirrors of each other, with an upper and lower berth, a seat facing the berths, and a basic bathroom, very like those found on American trains. Not being in first class, Jordan probably had a basin, but would have to wander down the passage for the head.

"What do you think of Lieutenant Jordan?" the countess asked, sitting on my berth.

I sat on the seat, facing her.

"Judging by his ring, he's married," I said.

She gave me her tolerant look.

"He seems to be what he is," I said. "I didn't detect anything that didn't add up."

"No," she agreed. "Nor did I."

I could tell there was something she wanted to say, but she alternately stared at me and at the floor.

"I want to stay with you tonight," she said, "but I am afraid that Lieutenant Jordan will knock on my door."

"I thought you made an impression on him," I said.

"It's not funny," she said. "I was trying very hard not to."

"By asking him all sorts of questions about the wonderful

things he did, people he saw, and places he'd been?" I teased.

She shrugged.

"What else could I do?"

"I am sure you can handle yourself if he comes knocking," I said.

"And that's why I need to be in my cabin when he comes," she said. "If I'm not there, things could get complicated. For you, as well as me."

She was right. I could see that, though the idea of lying with her on a gently moving berth, however narrow, was an enchanting idea.

"Will you give me my Beretta back?" she said.

It was the last thing I expected her to say, and I had no reply.

"I don't think Lieutenant Jordan will make trouble, but I don't feel safe," she said.

She spoke calmly, and I understood her request. I could also hear, in the back of my mind, someone from the Judge Advocate General's corps asking the question, "You knew that the countess had shot Sergeant Borroughs, but you gave her the pistol back, with ammunition?"

I took the gun out of my suitcase, where I had slipped it

behind the lining. I took the clip from its separate location, and removed all but two bullets, and gave her the two pieces, individually.

"Here. Give it back to me in the morning," I said. "It hasn't been cleaned since you last used it. I'm sure you have cleaning tools."

"In my make-up bag."

Chapter XXI

From my point of view, the night passed peacefully. Although the motion of the ferry was considerably more noticeable than the motion of the *Harrisburg* or the *Hartford*, it had the same soporific effect – though little rocking of the cradle was needed after the long day, several glasses of retsina, and two Metaxas.

No gunshots disturbed my slumbers, and I had slept too deeply to dream until daylight shone through my port-hole.

I was half dressed and shaving when the countess knocked on my door. I spoke to her through the narrow gap that I had opened, but she stepped in and I had to open it the rest of the way. She was ready for the day, and wanted to walk around the deck.

"I hate having nothing to do," she said.

"Have you cleaned the Beretta?" I asked.

She opened her handbag and handed over the pistol and clip without comment. I checked to ensure there were two bullets still in the clip, and slipped them in my suit-case. I'd put them somewhere different when she wasn't around.

"I think you'd better have this, too," she said, fishing in her handbag.

She handed over a brass casing.

I gave her a look of bored exasperation, but realised, perhaps for the first time, that her attention to detail had the hallmarks of a professional. I put it in my pocket, and would look after it. It was evidence; evidence of my complicity as well as of her murder.

She watched me finish shaving like a child watching her father. From the look on her face, I suspected that's what was in her mind, too.

"When do we get to Brindisi?" she asked.

"Eight o'clock tomorrow morning."

"What are we going to do until then?" she asked.

Her face then lit up.

"I know," she said. "Let's see how much money we can win from Lieutenant Jordan!"

We laughed.

"That would be hard for him to explain to the consul," I said. "I gather he didn't come to visit last night?"

She gave me a coy look.

"Now, that's the sort of question I wouldn't usually answer," she said. "But, since I brought it up in the first place, I'll tell you. No, he didn't."

We went up on deck. There were few people up there apart from those who had slept on the benches, or in the main saloon. Sleeping was not allowed in the cafeteria, but it was all right to pass out from too much drink for a few hours.

It was possible to walk completely around the ferry outside, but it did mean going down to a lower deck and up again at the bow. We did two circuits before standing on the port side and looking towards the sun.

"When will you find out if you're going home?" the countess asked.

"Why do you always think that I know more about what's going on than you do?" I asked.

She didn't answer, but watched the coastline.

It was how we spent most of the day. We ate Greek lamb and fish dishes, refreshing salads, and drank several bottles of retsina and Demestica, not to mention the rounds of Metaxas after dinner, and too much Greek coffee.

I wrote up my journal, recording times, dates, and conversations. I told the others I was writing a short story, and had to make up a plot about Sherlock Holmes and a chess match. Both Jordan and the countess were suitably unimpressed, and didn't ask further questions.

In the afternoon, we did have an attempt at fleecing Lieutenant Jordan, but in the end, I was the one who lost the most money. The countess, of course, won.

When the game finished, I took my journal to lock in my cabin, and brought the book I was reading, and one other back on deck.

Jordon was ordering some lemonade from the bar, and the countess was alone, her head back, and her face in the sun.

She sat up, and put on her dark glasses when she heard me approach.

"Hiding from me?" I asked, as I sat on the bench opposite her.

"I need some sun, or I'll look like a – *raton laveur*," she said, unable to find the English word, and drawing circles around her eyes with her fingers.

"Here, I brought you something," I handed her one of the books I'd brought up. "It's in English, but I thought you might like it."

"*Sunlight on Cold Water*," she said, musing. "Ah, Françoise Sagan! *Merci bien*!"

Lieutenant Jordan joined us, and gave a lemonade to the countess.

"Sorry, didn't know you'd come back up," he said.

I waved my hand indicating it didn't matter.

"Where are you from?" he asked, and we had the same conversation that I had had with Rodgers in Calcutta, Bowker in Bombay, and Mackenzie in Cairo. I didn't mind because it meant that he wasn't asking about my work on the *Harrisburg* and *Hartford*, the countess, or what we were running from.

While we talked, the countess read. Jordan was from Connecticut, a small town in the west of the state that didn't share the affluence usually thought of with Greenwich, Stamford, and Old Saybrook.

"Apart from the prep school, which is the other side of the Housatonic River from where I lived, there's nothing in Kent. I was happy to leave it," he said.

As he spoke, his description sounded a lot like Centerburg, and we shared the woes of small town life.

"I was decent at baseball," he said, "and I grew to like fishing."

"Do you ever fish in Greece?" I asked.

"Thought about it," he said, "but I've learned to sail with one of my friends. I really like that. You know how it is, though, just as I get good at it, I'll get sent somewhere with no water."

"Are you expecting a cut?" I asked.

"It's likely, though I've enjoyed my time here," he said. "I was able to have my wife move over for the last year. It's not a lot of fun for her, but it's better than being home alone."

He was curious about shipboard life, and confessed that on the way back, he'd probably sleep on one of the benches in the sun all day.

Before we went in for supper, we all walked around the deck three times.

Our meal was enjoyable, but we'd reached the point where we didn't feel the need to talk, and perhaps because of the fresh air, or perhaps because of the drink, we turned in around nine-thirty.

I was just about to slip under the sheet when there was a knock on the door.

I'd expected it to be Jordan with the next set of orders for me, and instructions regarding the countess, but it was the countess herself.

She was still dressed, and pushed my door open and walked in as soon as I answered it.

"What's wrong?" I asked.

She didn't answer, but sat on the seat near the port hole, and looked at her reflection in the glass, then turned to me.

"You were glad it was me at the door, weren't you?" she asked.

"Yes, of course."

"No; there's no 'of course' about it," she said. "What you don't realise is that I am not good for you."

I started to protest, but she cut me off.

"What you don't know, and I can't let you discover too late, is that I don't feel anything," she said.

"For me?"

"No, Bill, for *anything*," she said. "Three days ago, I killed a man, and walked onto a plane as though I'd just had a coffee. The things I've done, I was able to do because I don't feel anything: fear, remorse, love."

Again, I was about to say something when she shook her head.

"Please understand that this is not the way I *want* it to be; it's the way I am."

I was sitting directly opposite her, and looked straight in her disconcerting eyes.

"You're bruised," I began.

"I'm. . . *damaged*," she retorted.

"Look what you've been through, and what you've been asked to do," I argued. "Of course, it will deaden you, but not forever.

"I'm not going to psychoanalyse you, but you've stopped living in a war zone now; no one is going to ask you to do dangerous, or murderous things. You were only recently widowed when this began – you never had the chance to grieve properly."

She made no reply, and I doubted my words were getting anywhere.

"What about the other night? Not the love-making, but your tears? Surely you were feeling something?" I said. "Even if you were just feeling sorry for yourself, that means something."

She shrugged.

"All I know is that I am cold, and lonely. Can I stay here? With you, or in the upper berth, I just don't want to be alone."

She took off her shirt and skirt, and got into my berth. She lay on her side, back against the bulkhead, and reached across my chest when I climbed in.

"Countess," I began softly.

"Shhh. It's probably our last night, and I don't want you

to be disappointed," she said drowsily, and fell asleep.

☙

I was awoken by knocking on the door. There was daylight coming through the port hole. The countess was no longer next to me, and her clothes were gone. It was about six; we were due to dock in two hours.

Fumbling with the lock, I opened it to see Lieutenant Jordan standing in front of me. He was shaved and dressed.

"The countess isn't in her cabin," he said.

I stepped back and started to dress hurriedly while pretending not to notice that Jordan inspected my cabin and checked the head, too.

We went to the main deck.

"I'll go this way," Jordan said, and I walked around the other, doing the usual circuit. We met at the bow and shook our heads.

Next, we went into the cafeteria, and found the countess sitting at a table by the window, drinking a coffee and reading her book.

"I'm trying to finish it before we land," she said.

"Lieutenant Jordan thought you'd jumped overboard, or stolen a lifeboat," I said.

"And leave such charming company?" she asked, smiling.

"I'll get some coffees," Jordan said.

As soon as he had his back to us, the countess put her book down, leaned across the table, and whispered sharply.

"Why was he looking for me? I'm not his prisoner?!"

That had not occurred to me. There was no reason to wake the countess before seven.

"I reckon that he was trying to find out if you were with me," I said. "He could get me court martialled for conduct unbecoming, and earn some points for himself."

"I told you I didn't trust him," she said, still angry.

She returned to normal when he arrived with the coffee, and spoke easily.

I got myself some breakfast, as when we'd eat next was a great unknown. I got the countess some fruit and yoghurt as well as food for myself. I wanted to give Jordan and the countess some time, if they had anything to say to each other. If he had a hidden agenda, I had no idea what it was, and I thought he was basically up-front, if intrigued by the countess. He'd be completely infatuated if he knew that epithet.

When I returned to the table, Jordan was absorbed in his coffee, and the countess in her book. At least he was still alive.

"Are you going to eat?" I asked.

"No, I'll get something in Brindisi after I've handed you over," he said.

His language sounded like that of a sheriff.

I ate my breakfast in silence, as the countess continued to read.

"I'm going to find out when we're due to arrive," Jordan said, and left us.

"How late do you think we're going to be?" I asked the countess.

"An hour," she said. "Neither country is known for its timekeeping. I don't mind; this is pleasant enough, and is likely to be better than what follows; but when you finish, let's go outside."

It was chilly in the shade, but in the sun, comfortable enough. We walked around the aft deck, watching the coastline pass before settling on a bench in the brightness of the morning.

Lieutenant Jordan joined us a few minutes later.

"We're half an hour late," he said.

"Not bad after a two-night run," I said. "We left fifteen minutes late. It's nicer sitting out here than it will be on a train or in a car, which will be what we're facing. I'm going to get my book."

I went down to my cabin, and realising I hadn't shaved or finished packing, did both before returning to the deck. I found the countess alone.

"Where's Jordan?"

"He asked too many questions, so I threw him over the side," she replied, not looking up from her book.

"What time did you leave last night?" I asked. "I didn't feel or hear anything."

"Sleeping draughts have that effect on people," the countess said, still not looking up.

I was about ask if she really had done that, but suddenly realised what she was doing.

"I don't think of you that way, Countess," I said.

She looked up, and took off her dark glasses.

"Don't you? I think you do. You see me as a Hollywood *femme fatale* – no, you said it yourself, I'm the bride who wore black, seeking her revenge."

She put her dark glasses on again, and went back to her book.

I saw Jordan approaching, so my reply to the countess went unsaid.

"What do you know about Brindisi?" he asked me, sitting down.

"Not a lot. Ancient port; used since Roman times. Easy access to the Corinth Canal."

"In fact, it was used as a port by the Greeks," Jordan said. "It is also the beginning, or the end, if you prefer, of the Appian Way."

"A summer project for you," I said. "How long do you think it would take to walk it?"

"It's about three hundred miles, say twenty miles a day, throw in a few days for sight-seeing and rest, three weeks should do it," he said.

"You like walking?" I asked.

"Yes, but I don't think I'd want to do three weeks of it," he said. "My wife and I walked from Athens to Marathon last year. We tried to use paths and back roads, so it wasn't particularly direct. We did it in four days; the army of the time might have done it in two."

He continued talking about walking holidays. To me, he had a sensible approach, enjoying what he saw, not pushing for distance for the sake of it. He threw in tips on footwear, maps, what to carry and what not to bother with. By the time he finished, he could have signed me up for his walk from Athens to Corinth (three days).

At eight o'clock, he and I went down to get our cases, and the countess'. Already there was a line of suitcases and other baggage lined up along the edge of the deck near to where the gangway would be.

We could feel the ship slowing, and we were passing more traffic that had emerged from the harbour.

Before we returned to the main deck, Jordan stopped me.

"Why does a journalist need an escort back to France, and why didn't you just fly from Athens?" he asked. "Okay, it's none of my business, but I've been trying to figure her out since I met her."

"So have I, and I met her last October."

Chapter XXII

The *Eirene* docked at about 0845. While hardly a luxury cruise, it was restful after the more frenetic travel we had endured, but I felt it gave the countess too much time to think.

As we stood on the deck with our luggage, I scanned the pier, and saw an American Navy lieutenant waiting for us holding a briefcase. The system continued to work.

"My fate is in that case, isn't it?" the countess asked.

"Probably."

"What's the worst it can be, do you suppose?"

"That I am ordered to kill you," I said.

She looked down and watched the gap between the ship and the pier close. Then, she looked up.

"I could take it from you," she said.

I smiled at her.

"It won't come to that," I said.

Lieutenant Jordan was the first of us down the gangway, and he headed straight for the lieutenant. They saluted, identified themselves, and waited for us to catch up.

"Lieutenant Gallagher, this is Miss Françoise Mauriac," Jordan said. "And this is Lieutenant Bradley."

Gallagher smiled at the countess and greeted her. She did not extend her hand. He glanced at me, obviously not pleased that I wasn't in uniform.

Lieutenant Jordan lost no time in taking the folded sheet of paper from his pocket and giving it to Lieutenant Gallagher to sign, officially transferring responsibility for the safe passage of the countess.

"Miss Mauriac, I trust your return to Toulouse will go smoothly from here," he said.

The countess thanked him, and again, declined to extend her hand.

"Enjoy your boat ride, Lieutenant," I called to him as he departed.

"A word, Mr Bradley," Gallagher said to me when Jordan disappeared into the crowd.

"Excuse me, Miss Mauriac," I said to the countess, and she gave a regal nod.

Gallagher and I walked a few paces, and he opened his briefcase.

"These are your orders, and these are instructions for Miss Mauriac," he said. "I don't know what Jordan was talking about Toulouse for. She's certainly not going there.

"As you have accompanied her throughout her journey, would you like to go over the details of her trip and other arrangements with her?" he asked. "I will, but you might have a rapport."

"It's all right, sir, I'll do it. It makes sense," I said.

"What was the Toulouse bit?" he asked, casually.

"It's her cover story, sir. I can tell you, if you like."

"It's her future in the next few hours that concerns me," he said. "Once we've dropped her off, we can both go back to Naples."

I opened my orders and read them. We were taking the countess to a village called Stigliano, and then I was to proceed with Lieutenant Gallagher by train to Naples, and report to the British Consul.

"We'd better make a start, Mr Bradley," Gallagher said. "I've got a car and a driver."

"Why Stigliano?" I asked him.

"Nothing to do with us," he said. "The British are running this show."

Gallagher took the countess' suitcase and we went to the car where Yeoman Third Class Kornic waited patiently. He stowed the bags, and the countess and I got in the back seat, while Lieutenant Gallagher rode shotgun.

In the car, the countess, complete with dark glasses that she'd worn since leaving the ferry, looked out the window while I opened her instructions and read them. She showed no interest, but would accept them fatalistically.

The first page was addressed to me.

Dear Lieutenant Bradley,

You will have orders to accompany the countess to the remote village of Stigliano where a house has been prepared for her. There is also a housekeeper, Sra Rastelli. The enclosed instructions detail what the countess is permitted to do and not do.

There are details of a bank account and she will receive payments as long as she remains in Stigliano. Mrs Rastelli will advise us of the countess' well-being, which will no longer be your concern.

The consul in Naples will give you orders and tickets for London where we will meet for your debriefing before your return to the United States.

I have been asked to inform you of your early separation from the Navy, with effect from 1 June, and of your promotion to first lieutenant. May I offer you my congratulations, but I understand that this promotion is essentially awarded for continued respiration.

You may wish to pick up your new insignia while in

Naples, though you will have no chance to wear them in London.

Yours sincerely,

There was the characteristic large "H" followed by an indeterminate scrawl.

I folded the letter and put it back in the envelope.

"Anything interesting?" the countess asked with feigned indifference.

"Have you ever heard of Stigliano?" I asked her.

She shook her head.

"It's your new home," I said. "You have a house, a house keeper, and a bank account. You also have an Italian passport."

"That's nice," she said with the same detachment. "Is there anything in the bank account?"

"Yes, and you will receive a stipend. I don't know how much."

"Anything else?"

"Yes, I've got a promotion, and I'm going home."

I handed her the envelope with Hawthorne's letter and her instructions. She took it without a word, then turned to look out the window again.

୨୦

We drove in silence for more than an hour. I hated the idea that these last hours with the countess were not private, but who knew what she thought.

She had made no mention of her visit to my cabin the previous night, or about her inability to feel any emotions. The truth was that regardless what she felt, or didn't feel, I felt close to her. It was hardly surprising, she was the only female that I'd spoken to in months, and that I wasn't overly concerned about her murderous activities was further evidence that this was an infatuation born in the pages of spy fiction. The countess would remain an enigma whom I'd never forget.

"We're coming into a village called Scanzano Jonico," Lieutenant Gallagher said, turning towards us. "We can have a rest stop, and a coffee, or a cold drink, but we must press on. We're about half way."

We parked near a small hotel that had a café on the pavement. When we sat down, I wanted to order a chrysanthemum tea.

"We're only a few miles from the sea," Gallagher explained. "We've been following the arch of the foot of Italy, but will now turn north and get into the mountains."

I told Gallagher of my separation, and promotion. He said he'd take me to the BX in Naples for my railroad tracks. We chatted about the Navy; he'd had sea duty on the carrier *John F. Kennedy,* and was quite happy to have shore duty in Naples.

While we chatted, and waited for the coffee, the countess walked around and went into the hotel.

"Is she all right?" Gallagher asked.

"She's not a flight risk," I said. "I'm an escort, not a guard. We worked together in Saigon for the past five months."

"But I gather you're not working for the Americans in this?" he said.

I explained without going into detail, and he quickly believed it was intelligence work (was it?) and stopped asking about it. He did want to know what Saigon was like, and was surprised to hear I lived shipboard, instead of on the base.

"I was quite happy to be at sea," I said.

I told him about ending up with a stateroom to myself.

"I'm starting to think you're dangerous to know."

We were back on the road within twenty minutes, and as he predicted, the land started to rise until we were winding our way further and further up.

Eventually, amid the nothingness of the mountains, small farms and houses began to appear, and we drove into

Stigliano. While there were inevitably some old build-ings, most of them seemed to be post-World War II con-crete and cinderblock of the unattractive variety.

We wound around the town, still climbing, until Kornic pulled up in front of a row of older houses facing down the mountain.

Kornic got out and went up the few steps to the front door and gave three sharp strikes with the knocker. An old woman, whom I took to be Mrs Rastelli, opened the door, and came forward to greet us.

We had all got out of the car, but Mrs Rastelli went direct to the countess, took her by the hand, greeted her in Ital-ian and English, and led her into the house. Kornic car-ried her suitcase in, and we followed.

We let the countess explore on her own, but followed Kornic to the top floor. The house was on three levels, with kitchen, dining room and a small bedroom, presum-ably for Mrs Rastelli, on the ground floor; a large sitting room, the whole width of the house, on the next floor, (first in English; second in American), with views over the tops of the houses across the street. There was also a study and small bedroom at the rear, and several bed-rooms on the top floor. The one over the main room, fac-ing the view would be the countess' bedroom.

It was sparsely, but fully, furnished, and what furniture

there was, was of a good quality. Should the countess want to decorate, there was ample opportunity, but as one who had lived with military furniture for more than a year, I thought the house was comfortable.

Lieutenant Gallagher and Kornic went downstairs, while I waited in the bedroom for the countess. The views were breath-taking, and showed vast areas of nothing but farms with the odd small village.

The countess came in, holding her instructions.

"Have you read them?" I asked.

"How long am I to stay in exile?" she replied. "Is it forever?"

"I don't know, Countess," I said. "Everything appears to have been thought of."

She nodded.

"I suppose it's very generous."

"Better than a cigarette and a blindfold."

She smiled sadly.

"One day, I might welcome that."

There was a knock on the door behind us.

"Sorry to disturb you, sir," Kornic said. "Lieutenant Gallagher says you have a train to catch, and we'd better leave soon."

"Thank you, Kornic. Tell Mr Gallagher I'll be right down."

We listened to him go down the stairs.

I took the countess' hand and put a paper with my address in Ohio into it. She sensed what it was because she closed her hand without looking at it.

"Good-bye, Lieutenant Bradley," she said.

"Take care of yourself, countess," I said, and turned to leave.

"Bill!" she called, and I turned around quickly.

"May I have my gun back?"

"It's in your bag, Countess," I said, and she smiled. "But, only use it on other people."

Chapter XXIII

And that was it. Or, that's what I told Hawthorne, and later, Osgood. It was plausible; the countess might feel abandoned, but she was safe. No one was going to prosecute her for espionage or murder.

As for me, yes, I'd miss her, but we weren't that close. Not really. One of those war-time things.

"No doubt you spent time wondering what might have been," Osgood said.

"Of course, I did," I admitted. "She had my address, if she were interested she'd write."

"And, she never did."

"She never did."

"So, just to tie things up, you waved good-bye and drove away. Then what?" Osgood asked.

I told him that Kornic drove us to the station at Pisticci where we caught the train to Naples. He would drive back down to the coast where he'd spend the night, and drive to Naples on a decent road the next day.

"Gallagher took me to a reasonable hotel in Naples, then

the two of us went for a big meal with plenty of Lachryma Christi, coffee and limoncello," I said. "Curiously, we hardly mentioned the countess, which was just as well. Drawing a line under that experience would take some time.

"The next morning, I presented myself to the British consul and received instructions to fly to London that afternoon. I was given the address of a modest, centrally located hotel," I continued.

"There was a letter from Hawthorne on the desk in my room giving me the address of an office in Whitehall, asking me to report at 1400 the next day. That would give me time to go to the embassy and see if I could get some money to buy more civilian clothes for my time in London."

"Had you received any money from us?" Osgood asked.

"It had been paid into an account at Holt's since October, but I didn't have details of the account until that afternoon. Fortunately, the Americans continued to pay me."

"Tell me about Hawthorne's debriefing," he said.

"I went to the MoD building and was given a note to meet Hawthorne here. He met me downstairs, and we came to a room like this," I said.

"Was there anyone else present?"

"No. For three hours, I told my story, and was questioned, fairly closely on some parts of it. What surprised me was that he took no notes."

"That was Hawthorne," Osgood said.

"I concluded that the room was bugged, and I was being taped," I said.

"If only you had been; we wouldn't have to do this today," Osgood said.

"Are you recording this?"

Osgood gave me a bored look, then said, "No."

"What aspects did Hawthorne most closely quiz you on?" he continued.

"Three things in particular," I said. I knew this as I had written about it, among other things about *l'affaire de la Comtesse* in a separate journal, which I had told neither Hawthorne or Osgood about. "First, any indications that the countess might be disloyal or conflicted in her loyalty.

"Secondly, about Colonel Myerson. He seemed concerned at the coincidence of meeting him at the beginning and the end of my time in Saigon.

"Finally, about Borroughs," I said. "You've questioned that yourself. Hawthorne was looking for any explanation of his attempt to kill the countess, and me."

Osgood pulled his hand over his mouth in thought. I thought he was beginning to look tired; perhaps he was just bored.

"Let's take them in order," he said.

"The first one is easy," I said. "The closer to the end, the more the countess appeared uneasy about what she was doing. Once I knew some of it, I could see why. However, she never said she wished she wasn't doing it, or expressed any anger about it."

"You're sure of that?"

"She was an unhappy, and perhaps disturbed, young lady, but she seemed to have a strong sense of duty. Whether that was to her father, or the British, Americans, or whoever else might be pulling the strings, it was very strong.

"I also believed that because she never gave me any indication about how she was getting her instructions for our meetings," I said. "I was giving her one type of instruction, but I never did know how she knew when and where to meet me.

"Regarding Colonel Myerson, I was surprised to see him before leaving Saigon, but it was consistent with what he had told me in October," I said. "It was also typical of the way people run into each other in the military. After Hawthorne asked about it, I gave it more thought, but didn't come up with anything suspicious."

"Do you know what happened to him?" Osgood asked.

"No."

"You never thought to look him up on the internet?"

"No. He didn't surface in any of my subsequent work; anyway, by the time the internet was around, I'd long lost interest. I assumed he eventually retired and went back to Colorado to run a buffalo burger franchise."

Osgood refrained from scolding me for frivolity.

"Borroughs," he said.

"This was the real mystery," I began. "Throughout the time he'd been my driver, he'd been professional in every way. Courteous, affable when the occasion called for it; cautious, and a good driver, in that he watched the streets and buildings carefully for anything suspicious. I'd given him books, and we'd talked about fishing . . . ."

After all these years, the sight of the dead Borroughs, pistol in his hand, was vivid, and as shocking as it was that morning.

"I didn't doubt the countess once she'd handed over her pistol so easily," I said. "There was less than a second between the time I heard the shot and the time I turned around and saw Borroughs. She could not have staged it."

"Did you ever reach a conclusion?"

"Not really," I admitted. "My first thought was that neither of us was supposed to get on that plane, but there was no surprise when we did. All the links in our travels worked perfectly, and could not have done so at so short a time had the official plan been to kill us. Apart from that, we could easily have been killed *en route*.

"There was only one real conclusion: Borroughs was working for someone else. The North Vietnamese, or Viet Cong, was the obvious option, but once the countess told me about all the money being removed from the country, then the possibility of a contract killing opened up. However, I never found any evidence for that. If the countess knew, she didn't tell me, or have the opportunity to."

The waiter appeared and removed the tea things.

"The usual, sir?" the waiter said.

"Two," Osgood replied, then turned to me.

"Nearly done," he said. "I want you to tell me any thoughts you may have had, at the time, or since then, that might complete the picture."

I smiled at him. It wasn't a friendly smile, more a conspiratorial one. Osgood was civilised, yet his seemingly casual interviews turned up subtle inconsistencies that could be exploited, and ultimately achieve the agency's objectives.

"When Hawthorne finished his debriefing, which went on for four days, but only in the afternoons, I was ready and anxious to go back to the United States and begin my 'real life'," I said. "It was in the last half hour of the final day when he asked if I might be interested in extending my service to the agency.

"I was stunned. I hadn't done anything remarkable, and felt I had pretty much bumbled through the whole assignment. He said he thought I might make a better analyst than operative, and set out his proposition.

"He told me to go back to America and think about it, but to be back in London at the beginning of June, once my active duty with the Navy was complete. You know most of the rest of that.

"I did have a thought on the plane the next day that Hawthorne would be on his way to Stigliano to debrief the countess in the guise of Melville."

"Did you ask him?"

"No, but I inferred it from the odd comment he made when I returned to London in June, and we were tying up the loose ends. He indicated that she had been debriefed, if not by him, then by someone else.

"I worked for him until he retired four years later. Saigon and South Vietnam had fallen, and the world moved on."

"Did you ever hear from the countess?"

"No."

"How did you feel about that?" he asked.

"I got over it. I got married around the time of Hawthorne's retirement, and you took over."

"So why have they got us going through all this again?" Osgood asked.

"I can only think that the people involved are now in sensitive jobs, and revelations by the countess could be embarrassing," I said. "It could be about the money, or the operations to repatriate it. Or, it could be that someone who gave orders to kill is now an MP for a Home Counties' constituency; or possibly up for a cabinet seat, or a defence contract.

"Did you come up with anything?" I asked.

The waiter arrived with two gin and tonics, and a small bowl of nuts.

"Pretty much that. Someone is nervous, and for some reason the countess wants to come to England," he said. "She's entitled to, and, frankly, I can't see a reason why she shouldn't. She's kept her mouth shut for four decades. She's had ample opportunity to sell her story, or make trouble, and she hasn't."

"I never thought she would," I said. "She was clever and

attractive, but she had the oriental disposition of not rocking the boat, and accepting one's lot."

"Something the British used to have," Osgood observed.

"As you say; so, why does she want to come now? Well, she's over seventy; the streets of Stigliano are very steep; the house is on three floors, and she's sick of the view. She probably wants a nice flat in St John's Wood, and a reliable supply of gin and tonic," I said, reaching for my glass.

"Cheers," said Osgood, raising his.

Pausing to enjoy that first sip, I sensed that Osgood wasn't done with me yet.

Putting his glass down, he said:

"I want you to find the countess."

"Osgood, I'm retired. Send someone young to look for her," I protested.

"No," he said more firmly than I expected. "I need *you* to do this."

"Why?"

"Because the countess will let you find her."

∾

Well, who can ever object to a trip to Italy, especially at someone else's expense? I asked if I could take my wife, which Osgood said would not be a proper use of government money. We agreed, eventually, that I would be given an allowance to travel first class, but if I spent it on two less expensive tickets, then that would be acceptable, or at least not noticeable.

Given the discounts available to those over sixty, and the low prices for short-notice travel – especially at this time of year – I was able to secure two first class tickets for roughly the allowance I had for one. The hotels were not a problem since on the continent they charge for the room, not the number of people. Finally, since no one knew where the countess was, or how long it would take to find her, expenses were elastic.

The only possible cloud on this junket was that my wife had very mixed feelings about Italy, but I thought this could be solved by going via Paris.

We were both healthy and reasonably fit, so we would enjoy the trip.

Osgood was right about the countess letting me find her if she were around. She had no reason not to trust me, and Osgood thought she might even enjoy travelling with me again after forty-five years, but asked how my wife would feel.

Those months flitting between Yankee Station and Saigon to have coffee and drinks with an MI7 operative were probably the most exciting of my life, apart from my college days.

In the intervening years, the myths have replaced the reality; what seemed noble then looks like folly now; and what was revealed so clearly as a bad idea then, has been repeated several times since.

And, what of the countess; young and alone, but safe, on an Italian mountain?

I walked back to my flat near Russell Square. It was a balmy spring evening, and there were crowds of people along the route, all headed home. I rehearsed in my mind how I was going to put this trip to my wife, she didn't like flying, so we'd book trains, and sweeten the trip with the stop in Paris.

Gemma was in the sitting room with a glass of sherry and the evening paper when I arrived.

"Have you had a beastly day?" she asked after I kissed her. "You were gone for ages. Doesn't Osgood know you've retired?"

I poured myself a sherry, even though I'd spent much of the day drinking. I sat in a worn, but comfortable armchair near her.

"He agreed to pay, in the end," I said.

"And so he should," Gemma said. "I don't know how you

stuck it for so long."

"It was interesting work," I said, defending my career as an intelligence analyst.

The trouble with that sort of work is once you've stopped, you're completely redundant. Your one asset – knowing what's going on – is gone very quickly. Unless there is some old case – in which event you are invaluable, as long as someone remembers you're still alive – all you're good for is hospital committees, and being a school governor.

"You've got something else to tell me," Gemma said, putting her glass down, and leaning forward.

She always could read me, and it was probably just as well, as it avoided too many secrets. While I was never indiscreet, she knew when something was bothering me.

"He's asked you to do something, hasn't he?" she asked with a voice that made denial an impossibility.

"He wants me to go to Italy," I said.

She softened a little.

"Well, that's not too bad," she conceded. "Where, and for how long?"

"I'm supposed to find someone," I said. "It might take a while, but it shouldn't be dangerous."

She laughed.

"You're still trying to pretend that you're a spy," she laughed. "I don't expect you can tell me who you're looking for."

"Actually, I can," I said, and she looked at me with interest. "He asked me to find you."

Chapter XXIV

All right, I know. That's *not* fair. In writing this account, I have to confess that I have applied Dr Fagin's observation about schoolmasters, and tempered discretion with deceit, but after all, that is part of the game we're playing.

Gemma laughed, but then stopped suddenly, and her eyes widened.

"Really? Is that what he wanted to talk to you about?" she asked.

After decades of being settled, and content, she suddenly looked frightened.

"Isn't it over? After all this time?"

I knelt by her chair.

"Not yet. Osgood agreed that you could come with me, and I will need your help," said as reassuringly as possible.

She seemed mollified, but at about three in the morning, she woke me up and wanted to know more.

"How are you going to 'find' me?" she asked. "Do I have

to go back to that grim village?"

I told her that I'd related the whole story to Osgood, except about how and when she left Italy, and a few details of a personal nature.

"What about Borroughs?" she asked.

"No one knows anything about Borroughs," I said. "The Americans never made anything of it, so, they must have reckoned he was on someone's payroll besides theirs."

"I still worry about that one," she said.

She was holding me the way she always did, and I stroked her hair in the way that seemed to soothe her.

"No one is looking for you for anything that happened there."

She nodded, but I don't think she was convinced.

"When do we go?"

I glanced at the clock.

"I guess, tomorrow. I'll make the arrangements in the morning."

I said good-night to her, but she had already gone back to sleep.

છ

When I got back to America in 1973, there was already a letter from the countess waiting for me. I was delighted and excited, but delayed opening it, and the pile of other mail that had arrived in my absence, until I'd had a long visit with my parents and a big meal, met with friends and called distant relatives.

Finally, I was able to retreat to my room, and open the countess' letter.

Its contents were disappointing, but by morning, I realised it was all she could have written. She thanked me for looking after her; she said she was well and for the moment enjoying the quiet of Stigliano, and Mrs Rastelli's cooking. She hoped I was well and would soon make a happy civilian life for myself. She concluded with what I came to see as a sad little line, "I hope you will want to write to me."

She signed it three times: Gemma Linh Sargent Goddard, Françoise Mauriac, and The Countess.

I resisted the urge to write back immediately, and decided to do so only when I had an address in London, which was several weeks later. Through agency connections, and the money that had been accumulating at Holt's, I was able to lease the apartment near Russell Square where we now live.

Though I worked for Hawthorne, I seldom saw him. I was surprised to find other Americans on the team; some were ex-military, others were on loan from the State Department, and some recruited from other sources. To say the least, it was an eccentric assortment, and followed less than conventional methods. That, I was told, was part of the advantage of working for an agency that didn't exist.

I wrote to the countess (Gemma Linh!?) and gave her my address and said, of course, I wanted to write to her and wished her nothing but what was good.

We continued to write for three years. I wrote to her care of the local parish priest, to whom, I gathered, she had told much of her story. She didn't fully trust Sra Rastelli, though she had been very good to her. The countess wrote that she had told the priest that if he had any doubts about the nature of our letters, to open, and read them.

The rhythm of the postal service to Stigliano meant that we wrote to each other about once a month. Reading between the lines, the countess had no intention of staying up her mountain any longer than she had to.

In May 1975, I had a long poignant letter from her reflecting on the fall of Saigon, the end of her country, and what it would mean for her friends, her family home, and other places she had known well. Predictably, I was not uninvolved in the fallout from that event, and interviewed dozens of the more affluent and influential refugees, and analysing the meaning of what they told us.

In September of that year, several things came together. I had a letter from Gemma saying that Mrs Rastelli had died, and she had taken advantage of the gap in her supervision to leave Stigliano. She was back to living out of one suit-case, and was in a reasonably nice hotel in Naples. She was exploring the area, and was particularly taken with Capri.

Hawthorne had retired at the end of August, and moved to the south of France. There was no one who might rec-ognise the countess in England, apart from the odd naval officer, who would think she was Françoise Mauriac.

Faint heart, and all that, I took a week's holiday and went to Naples where I found the countess in a café opposite her once-opulent hotel.

She was simply, but elegantly dressed, and wearing her large dark glasses, but the first thing I noticed was that she was still wearing her gold choker.

She watched me with unrecognising interest as I sat down opposite her. A smile flooded her face for an in-stant, and then went back to her inscrutable look.

"I hope this doesn't mean you want me to kill someone else," she said.

What struck me, out of the context of Saigon, was the

distinctiveness of her accent. It had the French guttural slurring, but also clipped oriental features.

"I've come to take you home, Countess."

"Paris?"

"London."

"*Bon*. Is this official?" she asked.

"We can make it official, if you like," I said.

She looked at me, frozen, then took off the dark glasses, and dropped them on the table.

"*Vraiment*?"

"Absolutely."

Over dinner, she told me that the day after Sra Rastelli's funeral, she had left her house early in the morning, dressed in her *áo dài*, and wearing her dark glasses, took the bus to Pisticci, and then took the train to Naples. Ironically, by attracting attention, she preserved her anonymity. She changed into Western clothes before the train arrived, and checked into a hotel.

She had expected me to write with advice, not to arrive without notice and propose.

Getting her back into England took a little planning. I didn't want to risk flying, even though security then wasn't anything like as rigorous as it is today.

She had a stack of passports, all still valid, for Italy, France and the United Kingdom. Some existed in several names, from Françoise Mauriac (which had been her mother's name), to Gemma Sargent, and Gemma Sargent Goddard. We used the French passport to get into France, and the British one to get into Britain.

We took a train to Genoa, then a sleeper to Paris where we spent a day.

"Here we are, escaping again," she said, with more affection than I'd ever heard in her voice before.

The countess spent much of the day looking for her aunt, who had either moved or died. She couldn't find anyone who knew her.

The following morning, we took a train to Boulogne and connected to Folkestone. I said that we looked like an English couple on the way back from a dirty weekend in Paris, which amused her.

We married not long after our return to London.

One day when I came home, she announced that she'd got a job with BBC World Service, where she remained for thirty years, interrupted only by bringing up three children Thomas, Anne-Françoise, and Paul.

 C8

What Gemma and I now needed to figure out was, who

had initiated the message that the countess wanted to come home? And, who was that prospect supposed to frighten? I would also have to work out an explanation why I had been unable to find the countess.

We walked to St Pancras to catch the Eurostar. Gemma had not spoken of the trip since I had first told her what Osgood wanted me to do, but had been rehearsing her dealings in Saigon in her mind. Unlike me, she had no journal to refresh her memory, but I saw her making notes in a small hard-covered notebook that she'd picked up at the university bookstore. I was surprised to see that by the time we boarded the train, they ran to several dozen pages.

She had hardly spoken, but appeared calm, regardless of what she was thinking.

We were seated opposite each other in that quaint manner that Eurostar calls a "Club Duo." It wasn't until we were served our breakfast that she began to share what she'd been thinking.

"Can you find me a list of MPs on that thing of yours?" she said jabbing her knife towards my tablet.

I said I could.

"That might help," she said. "Because, at the moment all we know for certain is that the countess isn't planning on showing up in London and making trouble.

"I think you were right in your deduction that someone who has become wealthy, and can wield influence is trying to frighten an MP," she said.

"We have to hope it's that blatant," I said. "Anything subtle we couldn't find."

We finished our breakfast in silence. It was after our trays had been cleared, and we were drinking our coffee that I asked how I could convincingly claim not to have found her, when I reported back to Osgood.

"You'll just have to say I'm dead, darling," she said.

I found a list of MPs and passed the tablet to her. She read through it carefully, and made some notes in her book.

It's surprising that more people don't sit quietly without distractions because the brain fills up with such unexpected things; maybe not fully formed light-bulb moments, but sparks that can be encouraged.

As I developed my idea, Gemma was writing names down. Then, she sat back to think, and unexpectedly asked:

"Did you bring your journal with you?"

I said I had.

"Can you write a list of all the military people mentioned in it," she said. "British and American."

"Have you got an idea?"

"Maybe."

We took a taxi to our hotel, and unpacked, as we would be there for about two weeks. I looked out the window onto the Seine and the Louvre, and wondered why we didn't spend more time in Paris.

Our daughter, Anne-Françoise, lived near the Bois de Boulogne, and I knew Gemma was anxious to spend time with her. Whether Anne-Françoise was equally eager, I didn't know, but the promise of a sponsored shopping trip to Galeries Lafayette would probably tip the balance.

We walked down for lunch at a café on Île Saint Louis and enjoyed large glasses of wine.

"You are going to Stigliano?" Gemma asked.

"Yes. I've had an idea of how to make you safe while coming back with a story to convince Osgood," I said. "While I'm gone, you can work out who was pretending to be you."

After lunch, I visited the SNCF office to arrange trains to Stigliano, while Gemma worked through the list of military contacts I'd given her.

When I got back to the room, she was working at the desk, and there were sheets of paper all over the surface, on the floor and bed.

"Writing your memoirs?" I asked.

"It's a *triage* process," she explained. "I've separated the unlikely from the likely and most likely."

"You knew a lot more people than I did," I said.

"I wish I could remember more," she said.

I knew she felt that way, but in truth, her memory was remarkable, and I doubted she had forgotten anyone.

"Did you get your travel arranged?"

"I can get a sleeper to Milan leaving just after seven tomorrow evening, with a good connection to Naples."

"How will you get to Stigliano?"

"I'll hire a car. The more receipts I can give Osgood, the better. The train gets into Naples around eleven-thirty, and Stigliano is less than three hours from there."

"Where will you stay?" the countess asked.

"If you let me use my tablet, I'll book something. Three nights should do it, don't you think?"

"You could knock on every door in that time," she laughed. "I'm going to call Anne-Françoise. We can meet her for lunch tomorrow."

When she reached for the telephone, I snatched my tablet off the desk.

Chapter XXV

While it was wonderful to see Anne-Françoise, she and her mother talked non-stop in French, and I was barely able to keep up. As our children had no idea about their mother's early career as a government assassin, we couldn't tell Anne-Françoise much about why we were in Paris, or why I was headed to Italy. As it was, I could tell she was suspicious when I said I was in France on business. Gemma would never give away what we were really up to, but it introduced an element of awkwardness into our conversation.

"Daddy and I are here because we need to convince the British government that I have no intention of returning to England, and am probably dead," was the sort of line that belonged in television sitcoms, not coming out of the mouth of one's seventy-two-year-old mother.

Our children had accepted what we'd told them, and we'd woven a pretty convincing version of events. In that version, I had been in the US Navy, and I had done work for the Ministry of Defence, and went to work for them permanently. Gemma and I had met in Paris on my way

321

back to England, kept in touch, and were able to develop a more or less normal romance until we got married. All very respectable.

The children accepted it, and so did our friends. No one knew the truth, apart from those who we'd worked with in Saigon, and had helped us leave it. They were now our prime suspects.

෨

Stigliano was no more attractive forty years later than I'd remembered it. Indeed, it reminded me of what we said about Centerburg, Ohio, when I was in high school: the best view of Centerburg is the one in the rear-view mirror as you headed up Route 36 at sixty-five miles an hour. Alas, the roads in Stigliano didn't allow such speed.

The hotel was convenient, clean, and had good food and wonderful views. There aren't many strangers in Stiglino, and I did my best to be seen.

While the hotel owner was too young to remember the countess, I did tell him that I was working for the British government, and was there to find out if anyone remembered anything about the foreign lady who lived alone at the top of the town, and the day the strangers came to take her away. I said I'd be around for several days, and would be in various cafés, and would buy anyone with a story a drink or two.

I had decided that planting and fostering a false memory about the countess would make her untraceable, and give credibility to the idea that she was dead. And so, for three days, I sat in the growing warmth of an Italian spring, in various cafés and restaurants, reading, and buying drinks for strangers. And, oh, what they remembered about the countess!

I noted down all the conversations to give to Osgood.

"The sad beautiful lady. A widow, she came to our beautiful village to mend her broken heart. . . ."

"She hadn't been here a week before her reputation as a harlot was all over the valley. . . ."

"My wife, may she rest in peace, told me that she was a lonely young woman who, was friendly, but would never be drawn into conversation. . . ."

"Sra Rastelli said there were statues of daemons in the alcoves, and she had to dust them. . . ."

"Sra Rastelli was afraid to enter the house after dark. . . ."

"The only person who seemed to know her was our late parish priest, Don Lorenzo, a saintly man who baptised and buried all our families for thirty years. . . ."

"I don't spread gossip, but I heard she poisoned Sra Rastelli. . . ."

"It was no wonder the poor foreign lady didn't talk to

many people, Sra Rastelli gave her a lifetime of talk every week. . . ."

"She dressed like a whore; the teenaged boys and children were forbidden to go near her. . . ."

"We didn't know who the men were who came for her, but they had a truck like a police van – all black – and they bundled her down the steps of her house and threw her in the back. . . the house was vacant for years. . . ."

"They say they shot her in the woods. . . ."

"A body was found on the banks of Lago di Gannano after the spring thaw. She had been shot. . . ."

"Stabbed seven times. . . ."

"Thrown into the Agri, and washed up in the lago, ten kilometres away. . . ."

ᷣ

"By the time I left Stigliano, there was no doubt that you were dead," I told Gemma when I got back to Paris. "No future investigation would turn up anything of any sense."

"That's a relief, I suppose," Gemma said. "Though I'm not sure I like the idea of being remembered as a harlot, though the idea of teenaged boys being pulled from my sight is amusing."

"And Sra Rastelli? Did she have any help in leaving this world?" I teased.

"There are lots of things you can put into Italian food," Gemma said coyly. "I only killed when ordered to – or in self-defence."

We went out for a meal that evening, and talked about how she'd spent time shopping, visiting galleries with Anne-Françoise, and catching up on bits of family news that our sons hadn't got around to telling us. We were pleased to know that the three of them were in touch almost daily via email and Skype.

Anne-Françoise was a freelance writer working for a variety of publications, in print and online. She wrote about fashion, social issues, and the environment, but had recently found writing about financial matters more lucrative. With no set hours, she was able to spend time with her mother, and shop, while I was in Stigliano.

Gemma and I went for dinner at one of our favourite places, as it was our last night in Paris. We didn't talk about our projects, but about our children, and their present success and happiness. She told me about galleries she visited, and related that Anne-Françoise still had no regular boyfriend.

"She's too much like you," I said. "It's going to take some upheaval in her life to make her seek lasting companionship," I said.

"I just hope it's not too painful," Gemma said. "Lives are

complicated enough these days."

"And yours wasn't?"

"You don't notice it, do you? Whatever hits you, you just cope," she reflected. "It's harder when you watch it happen to someone else."

We walked along the river back to the hotel, and Gemma produced a bottle of brandy that she'd been enjoying in my absence.

When she'd poured, and we'd settled into the chairs by the window overlooking the river, Gemma related what she'd been up to.

"I know it was a sacrifice letting me use your tablet," she began.

Sacrifice, my eye! She had pinched it from my case when I wasn't looking, a fact I didn't discover until the train was leaving Gare de Lyon.

She took the stack of papers that I had last seen all over the room, along with her notebook, and put them on her lap.

"I think it is reasonable to assume that the person most frightened by the prospect of the countess returning would be someone British, while the person making the threat could be British, American, or something else altogether.

"Starting with that thought, I listed my British contacts; those who would most likely know what I was doing," she continued. "There were remarkably few. There are even fewer who are still alive. Where I could find it, I've put the date that people have died next to their names.

"It is also reasonable to think that those British people would be around our age. Anyone older wouldn't be particularly vulnerable, and would shrug off any allegation. So, it has to be someone who still *wants* something."

I thought all this was sound.

"Most people have quietly retired," she said. "There are one or two who stand out. One is the attaché who met us in Calcutta."

She looked at her list.

"Rodgers. Geoffrey Rodgers. Detached from the Royal Navy in 1976 as a lieutenant commander, and entered the Foreign Office," she read from her notes. "Served in the foreign office until he was about forty-five, then entered politics. Stood in several unwinnable seats, and then won when the coalition government came in, in 2010. He's now on the Intelligence and Security Committee. Any bad publicity could finish him, and ensure he never enjoys the touch of ermine."

"That's a good theory. What about the consuls themselves? In Bombay, and Calcutta; they may have known about you."

"Both dead."

We thought about this. While Geoffrey Rodgers might be a good target, who would want to stop him, and why? This was the real question, as Osgood would probably know who was worried. If my story about the disappearance and assumed death of the countess was strong enough, it may make whoever was in fear of her return to feel safe – unless the perpetrator tried a new tactic.

Light from the *bateaux mouche* came in the windows and wrapped around the room before passing, and we watched the fell of night embrace the city.

∞

Osgood wanted to see me as soon as I returned to London. He had signed off on a substantial amount in expenses, and no doubt had to answer to someone.

We didn't meet at his club this time, but in a pokey meeting room at the Ministry of Defence. A soldier showed me to the room where Osgood was waiting.

"This room is a bit below your paygrade, isn't it?" I asked him.

"Oh, just sit down, Bradley," he said. "I presume you have something to tell me."

I gave him a transcription of the interviews I did in

Stigliano. He flipped through the nearly dozen pages before beginning to read them more carefully.

"Is there some way of getting coffee?" I asked.

"Ask the soldier outside the door," he said, without looking up.

He read quietly for about a quarter of an hour, then began re-reading bits he'd marked the first time through.

"You really spoke to all these people?"

"I have the drinks' receipts," I said tapping the envelope I'd put in front of him.

He tossed the statements away from him.

"Was there a body?" he asked.

"Apparently so," I said. "The police in Stigliano had a thin file on the case. The body had been badly disfigured on its trip down the river, and was judged to have been in bad shape before entering it. Female, aged twenty-one to thirty; possibly a prostitute. No one claimed the body, or came to identify it."

"Sometimes we have to use negative evidence," Osgood said. "It makes people uncomfortable, but I concede there is a good argument for it being the body of the countess. The rest of the statements are rubbish, as you know."

He put the pages into the envelope with the receipts.

"Do you think the countess killed Sra Rastelli?" he asked. "They seem to think she did."

"The countess was certainly capable," I said. "I gather that poisoning was one of her accomplishments."

"But would she kill without being paid for it?" Osgood asked.

"She would if her life were in danger," I said, remembering Borroughs. "But, probably not by poison."

"Indeed," Osgood agreed. "So, who sent word that the countess wanted to come home?"

"I'm afraid I've drawn a blank on that one, but I think I know who would be concerned if she did," I said.

"Oh, yes, who's that, then?"

"Sir Geoffrey Rodgers."

Osgood gave no reaction, but was silent for just too long.

"You know I can't tell you," he said.

"You know you just did," I replied.

"So, who is disturbing his peace, and why?" Osgood said.

And I suddenly had an idea, and it went well beyond Sir Geoffrey.

Chapter XXVI

The interview with Osgood went on for another hour. I told him I couldn't explain the polarisation of opinion regarding the countess; how some thought she was a sad, gentle lady, while others saw her as Lucrezia Borgia.

I told him I had gone to see the house, which had been abandoned for years after the countess left, but was now restored and occupied by a family with many children. Of those men who thought she was promiscuous, no one admitted to having slept with her. Of those who had been teenagers, none of them remembered much about her, except she was foreign, and lived alone in a big house. None thought she was particularly provocative.

"My problem, Bradley, is that in spite of the probabilities, this is still unresolved, and I can't give up on it until it is," he said.

"Well, I've done my bit," I said. "I've been down memory lane, all the way to Stigliano. My advice to you would be to send word back via the route you received the request saying that it's perfectly all right for the countess to return whenever she wants."

Osgood looked uncertain.

"I can't do that," he protested. "The parliamentary committee would be furious."

"What can they do?"

"Cut off my pension, for one thing," he said.

"If you want to flush out the countess, calling her bluff is your best bet," I argued. "We can't follow an invisible thread back, and if the countess is dead, then whoever is behind this can't move any further. You're in the clear, old boy."

Osgood shot me a disapproving look, more for the "old boy" than the substance of the argument. He had no answer, and sank back in his chair.

"Cheer up," I said. "I'll buy you lunch."

જી

We had a very good lunch, which I put on my expenses, over which we didn't discuss the countess, her victims, or those others affected by her activities.

"You must come round one evening for dinner," I said. "Gemma is a good cook."

He regarded me sceptically.

"I'm sorry I wasn't more help," I said, but I've told you everything I know."

332

On the way home, I bought a bottle of champagne. Gemma was out when I got back. She was on several charitable boards, but I didn't know whether today was the hospital, the orphans, or the illiterate.

I spent the afternoon reading, and listening to the radio. I had the champagne glasses out, and the ice bucket ready when she returned. Gemma looked surprised when she saw them, and asked what the occasion was.

"I've solved the mystery of the countess," I said. "I worked it out, and it all fits, and makes sense."

I took the bottle from the refrigerator, uncorked it and poured.

"To my clever countess," I said. "You are *really* good."

She drank, but looked suddenly nervous.

"It came to me when Osgood and I were reviewing the motives and possible perpetrators. I didn't tell him, because I wanted to think it through," I said. "Now that I have, I see that it makes perfect sense."

Gemma took her drink and sat on the sofa.

"It must have amused you enormously to watch it all happen," I teased.

"I can't think what you're talking about," she said, but the look in her eye told me that I was right. "Now, are you going to tell me, or do I have to guess?"

I laughed, and refilled our glasses.

"Here's to you, Countess. You have the Ministry of Defence and MI7 running in circles," I said. "And you had me going, too.

"Who else would think of bringing the countess back after all these years? No one knew enough of what to say to get a message taken seriously."

I looked at her for any sign of acknowledging the veracity of what I said. There was none.

"What made me think of you, was that I thought of your father," I went on. "Richard Sargent was a great adventurer, but he would have hated his little girl being forced to become an assassin, especially on his behalf.

"Once I was able to confirm that he was dead, as reported twenty years ago, and that Hawthorne was also dead, there was really no one else left."

Gemma still gave no hint at the accuracy of my deduction, and I recognised traces of her look of inscrutability from when I still believed she was Asian.

"We have a clever daughter who is a writer who could easily send a note to the British embassy in Paris saying that the countess was now fully sick of Stigliano, and wanted to return to the UK, and could her safety be assured.

"However innocuous the note looked, it brought a department head out of retirement, and a senior analyst. Ironically, it also jeopardised the safety of the countess herself, for if she were discovered to be alive, and in England, who knows what the consequences might have been?" I said.

I found I was ready for another glass of champagne. I topped up Gemma's glass, and finished the bottle. I waited to see if she would break her silence. Eventually, she spoke. Her voice was calm, and gentle, and sounded very similar to the way I first heard her.

"Congratulations," she said. "You are right about just about everything. It was for a sort of revenge for my father that I set things in motion. I also wanted to know who knew what about me. As it happened, only you and Osgood appeared to know anything."

"It was a risk, Gemma," I said.

"I needed to know, and I wanted to be, shall we say, inconvenient," she replied. "I also thought you needed a diversion. You were getting bored."

I laughed.

"Next time, just suggest we go to the Cotswolds," I said.

"I needed to face a few things," Gemma said.

"Exorcise some daemons?"

"If you like."

"Did it work?" I asked.

"I had no purpose – purpose for myself – until we met," she said. "You made me feel that there was a real life somewhere. I had no idea you were going to be part of that life, then, but you were like a window that I could see it through."

"You had Paris."

"Yes, and that was wonderful, in ways, but not in all ways," she said. "It was mixed with the death of my mother, my marriage to Claude, and then his death. I was so without direction throughout that whole period. I married him in some sort of daze. I never regretted it, but we were only married for a matter of weeks.

"I don't know," she said wearily. "There are so many things I'd change."

"Gemma: I just relived that period, pretty intensely with Osgood's questioning, and I don't see what I – or we – would have – or could have – done any differently," I said. "Anyway, it's not a question of having regrets, because we were not fully culpable."

"That's what Don Lorenzo said, in Stigliano."

"You told him *everything*?" I knew she had confided in the priest to some extent, but this surprised me.

"I confessed it. I needed to; how else would I be able to live? He listened, and didn't judge. It took two days to get through everything – not two days continuously," she said with a smile. "Even I wasn't that bad.

"He simply asked me what I was going to do. I said I was going to be good, and try to do good," she said.

"And did that help?"

"Do you know what penance he gave me? One 'Hail Mary.' I did something I never do: I burst into tears, and sobbed the way I did with you that time. He took my hand, but didn't hold me, and sat with me in silence until I was back in control.

"Did it help?" she repeated. "It made the rest of my life possible."

I had lived with the countess for four decades, and – God and Gemma forgive me – never explored those dark times with her.

"But don't you see, you didn't need to," she said. "They were truly over; but those bureaucrats, puppet-masters, mandarins – whatever you want to call them – they were completely untouched. They were three, four, five, ten times removed from the reality of paying the money, mixing the poisons, or pulling the trigger. They hadn't said that one 'Hail Mary,' or ever apologised to me, and the other ordinary people whose lives they ended, or forever corrupted. And, they got you, too, my darling."

Now, it was I who was silenced. I sat and looked at her, remembering the time in Vietnam; of being sucked into the morass. But, I also remembered the births of Thomas, Anne-Françoise, and Paul, and learning, as all parents do, that there is always more love, and Gemma has so much to give, perhaps because of those troubled times.

"What I wanted most after all that was to feel safe," Gemma said. "I knew you were a good man, and that with you I would be. Loving you was a bonus."

I wasn't certain whether this was flattering or not, but she was still with me, so I wouldn't question it.

"I've given your friend Osgood a hard time, and may continue to do so," she began. "Why don't you invite him to dinner next week."

I smiled.

"Curiously, I suggested just this afternoon that he come around," I said.

"Good," she said, standing and taking the empty glasses to the kitchen. "Do you know what he likes to eat?"

"He's very fond of a good Indian curry."

She considered this.

"That will be perfect. There are lots of interesting things one can put in a curry."

The Countess Comes Home

The End

Did you enjoy *The Countess Comes Home*?

Entrusted in Confidence

Three more stories about the countess and Bill Bradley. Osgood and Bradley continue their work for MI7 and these stories focus on personal and political events, and Bradley's penchant for stumbling into intrigue. "The Countesses Secret," "The Brentano Affair," and "Bill Bradley Rides Again," take the reader through the corridors of power in Whitehall and through the streets of Paris, discovering secrets along the way.

By the same author:

Nantucket Summer

From the haunted residents of the darkened rooms of the unpainted Hardwicke mansion, Midwestern waitresses, and the retreats of the establishment, to the creeping, *nouveau riche* infiltrators with their oversized, post-modern houses and competitive spirits, *Nantucket Summer* is a memoir of those who summered on the wood-framed New England coast in the 1960s.

Wachusett

In the summer of 1876, the nation prepares to mark its centennial. Marion Easton travels from her Boston home to a resort hotel on Mount Wachusett in central Massachusetts where she joins her future in-laws and their family. However, as July 4 approaches, there is little to celebrate.

The Camels of the Qur'an

The death of a BBC journalist, a missing girl, and an unpublished novel, lead the reluctant David Powell into a labyrinth of Middle Eastern customs, politics and intrigue. Determined to discover if his friend's death was an accident, or murder, Powell finds his familiar reference points gone, and nothing quite what it seems.

Portland Place: A novel from Jane Austen's Lost Years

Jane Austen meets the Americans. In the "era of good feeling," Nora Woodruff finds herself in London for the first time, and encountering citizens of the new nation. Manners and attitudes conflict against a background of rising political tension.

On the Edge of Dreams and Nightmares

Winner of a Chill with a Book *Premier Reader's Award*

A tale of child-abuse, incest, madness and murder: Ligeia Gordon's solution to her deep psychological troubles is to infiltrate the life of the distinguished painter, Sir Nigel Thomas, an older man who has his own ghosts to contend with.

Watch for:

Undivulged Crimes

What do you really know about the person sitting next to you? The tales in *Undivulged Crimes* encompass the romantic, ghostly, satiric, and the simply disturbing. Set in the United States and Europe, these stories explore secrets from the dark side of ordinary people, from an historical curse, to fraud, deceit, and murder.

The Rock Pool

The power of a special place can become a lasting influence, and when combined with the experience of love, it is a potent mix. Nick Lucas' love for the unobtainable Sarah Hallam becomes the unwelcome center of his life.